JASON AND MARIGOLD

Samantha Arran

ARTHUR H. STOCKWELL LTD
Torrs Park   Ilfracombe   Devon
Established 1898
www.ahstockwell.co.uk

This is a work of fiction. Names, characters, places and incidents are
the product of the author's imagination and any resemblance to actual
persons, living or dead, events or locales, is purely coincidental.

By the same author:
Love never Fails
Unfailing Love

All proceeds from this book are
going to widespread chosen charities

ISBN 978-0-7223-3977-0
Printed in Great Britain by
Arthur H. Stockwell Ltd
Torrs Park   Ilfracombe
Devon

Chapter 1

He stood feeling and looking bored; he hadn't wanted to come to this party but his mother had begged him to. He would much rather have been walking his dog in the fresh air on Hampstead Heath after a day in the stuffy courtrooms, where he was a barrister preparing to be a Queen's Counsel.

Across the room he spotted a beautiful blonde standing on her own looking uncomfortable; he felt a pull of attraction for her, and when she moved to the balcony outside he followed her.

He introduced himself and asked, "Would you like a drink?"

She told him her name and said, "Thank you – I'm fine just yet."

"Have you come with anyone?"

"Yes, my aunt. I am supposed to be modelling this dress."

"Do you like modelling?"

"Not really, but my aunt has cared for me since I was eight; my parents and paternal grandparents were killed in a car accident. She put me through boarding school, university and finishing school in Paris. I don't know anyone here, so I am hoping to escape as soon as I have done my duty." She laughed.

Jason leant against the railing.

"Yes, I can sympathise. I didn't want to come, but my mother and aunt persuaded me, as it is a charity evening. I would much rather be on the heath.

I am a barrister and the courts are very stuffy in this hot weather; I'm hoping to escape also soon."

His mother, Lady Norton, appeared. "There you are, Jason!"

Looking at Marigold, she asked, "Are you enjoying yourself, Miss Carlisle?"

"Yes, thank you, Lady Norton."

"Right, I'll continue mingling. Dinner will be announced soon."

Jason ruefully looked at Marigold and said, "It appears we cannot escape yet."

"Not really."

"Have you just completed finishing school?"

"Yes," she laughed, "it's supposed to have turned me into a proper young lady."

"And has it?"

"My aunt will be disappointed if it hasn't. I'm now going into her dress business, in administration. I took business studies at uni, with computer graphics and hand art. I'm going to design outfits."

"Did you get a degree?"

"Yes, a first in all."

"Well done! Congratulations!"

"I took haute couture in Paris."

The dinner gong went.

"May I escort you?" Jason asked.

"Yes please."

Marigold's aunt came up. "I have been looking for you, Marigold. Are you mingling?"

Marigold made the introductions. Her aunt looked pleased.

"Very well, cherie. I am sitting with an old friend; he will be coming back with me, so please do not disturb us."

Marigold, blushing, looked at Jason.

When her aunt had gone, he asked, "Do you like living with your aunt?"

"This is really my first time as I have been away being educated. I have always spent all my holidays in France with my maternal grandparents or in Cornwall with my ex-nanny. I'm looking for an apartment now that I have completed my education – I don't want to be in my aunt's way. I will continue studying art and design."

Jason was pleased. He knew Marigold's aunt and of her many affairs.

They enjoyed their meal.

"Would you like a lift home?" (Her aunt and companion had disappeared.)

Marigold thanked him. "I will get a taxi," she added.

She suddenly felt very shy of him. He was tall – well over six

4

foot – lean with powerful shoulders, black curly hair, gorgeous green eyes and wonderful mouth – he was too good-looking.

She was a virgin and she was not used to being on her own with a man. She didn't know what he would expect of her.

"I will get you safely home, that is all, Marigold."

He understood. He felt strangely protective towards her, which was unusual for him.

He helped her out of his car and asked, "If you are free tomorrow evening, would you like a walk on the heath whilst we have this wonderful weather? Then what about supper outside a pub?"

"I would like that."

"Good! Is it all right for me to bring my dog?"

"I love dogs," she told him.

"Shall I pick you up at 7?"

"Yes, I will be ready."

"Thank you, Marigold. I have really enjoyed your company this evening."

She didn't know whether to shake hands, so she kept her hands down. Jason laughed and touched her nose. A thrill went through her.

"See you tomorrow, Marigold. You have nothing to fear from me."

She blushed.

He thought, 'Not yet!'

The next evening Jason came in an open-top sports car with his German shepherd in the back. The dog greeted Marigold in a very friendly manner. They set off. It was a glorious evening. They threw sticks for Nelson, walked and talked. Several people called out to Jason or waved, but didn't intrude on them.

He asked, "Would you like me to help you find an apartment? In my profession I have contacts." (He wanted to get her away from her aunt's lifestyle.)

"Yes please. I will be grateful for advice."

"I hope you'll be relaxed with me, Marigold. I suspect you are a virgin?"

Blushing, she nodded.

"You are like breath of fresh air."

Marigold told him, "I overheard some models discussing my aunt and one said that her latest companions are getting older and older – after so many affairs she is losing it."

"I am sorry you heard it in that way, Marigold. I'm afraid it is the truth; but, thankfully, you have been away from her and out of it. You are not responsible for your aunt, so hold your head high. May I ask how old you are, Marigold?"

"Twenty-three."

"I'm thirty-two. I have an apartment at home – my mother likes to make sure I eat properly." He laughed. "My twin brothers are at Cambridge University and my older brother is serving in Afghanistan."

They called at a country pub, sat outside, had a wonderful meal and drank spring water.

When Jason took her home he told her, "I have never enjoyed a walk more. Will you come with me again?"

"Yes please."

"What about Saturday morning – I haven't to work this one – and then lunch?"

Marigold told him how much she had enjoyed the pub meal and being near the river, where Nelson could enjoy himself too. Jason rang the pub and booked a table.

"By Saturday we may both have news of an apartment," he said.

"I hope so," Marigold replied.

Yvonne was waiting for Marigold to come home.

"Well done, darling, for having dinner with the millionaire! Are you seeing him again?"

"We are walking on Saturday morning and then having lunch."

"I'm delighted, darling; if we get into their circuit, our business will flourish. You have pleased me, Marigold."

Her heart sank.

"Tante [her childhood name for her aunt], I am not dating Jason. We are good friends. He knows I am a virgin."

"Yes, darling, but you have to lose your virginity sometime – why not with him? He would look after you, a man like him."

"What do you mean, 'a man like him'?"

6

"Darling, he will need sex to relax him when he has been in the courts all day coping with legal problems. I'm sure he has had affairs."

Marigold rushed to her room crying. Yvonne followed.

"Please, Marigold – I don't mean to upset you, but, darling, you are my responsibility and I want the best for you."

"I know you do, Tante. I will do some designing now – I have ideas buzzing in my head."

"Very well, darling. Don't work too late."

When Jason collected Marigold on Saturday morning he noticed she was quiet and withdrawn.

He asked, "What is it, Marigold? You are unlike yourself. Has someone upset you?"

"My aunt told me you have had affairs, and she advised me to give you my virginity, saying you will boost her business."

Jason swore and then apologised. He pulled over as soon as possible.

"Marigold, yes, of course I would like to have sex with you – any man would. You are beautiful and full of sex appeal. You are not aware of your pull. But, darling, we are friends and companions until you decide to take our relationship further. I promise you I will never ask you; I love just being with you. Yes, I have sown my wild oats, but I am not promiscuous; I have always used protection. Do you know what I mean?"

She nodded.

"Now, darling, let's get on to the heath. I have some news of a suitable apartment; but it is your choice, of course."

When they began walking, Jason told her about a new apartment he had heard of, and he said he had asked the estate agent to hold it until that day.

"May I take you this afternoon to view? When we have had lunch, I'll take you home to change and then pick you up later. Does this sound OK, Marigold?"

"Thank you, Jason – it certainly does; I need to get out of Tante's way."

Jason then took hold of Marigold's hand and asked, "All right?"

"Thank you, Jason – I am now."

He kept hold of her hand. He asked her about her designing, and she told him she was preparing for the October show.

"That's a long time away," he said, amazed.

"Yes, it takes months to prepare. I love working with different materials and colours. Would you like me to make you a tie?"

"Yes please. What colour?"

"What about pink with red spots on?" she teased.

"Don't you dare!"

Nelson came sniffing her left hand.

"Look how my dog loves you."

When Marigold arrived home her aunt was out, so Marigold left a note:

> Jason and I are viewing an apartment this afternoon. Please keep this evening free, if possible, to look at it, and then you and I can have dinner at Claridge's.

The apartment was perfect: it was on the second floor and it had one bedroom, a kitchen, a dining room, and a lounge with big windows, useful for Marigold's art and designing. All the rooms were spacious. In the entrance to the building there was a security office. Outside there was parking for cars, and a valet service was available. The apartment block was in a select area.

"I love it, thank you, Jason."

He gave her the estate agent's number; she rang and asked the price.

"Yes, that is satisfactory. When may I move in?"

She nodded to Jason, and he gave the thumbs-up.

"Thank you, Jason – it's lovely. I couldn't have found it alone."

"What are you doing this evening?"

"I thought I would bring Tante to see it, and then I will take her to Claridge's for dinner."

"Brilliant! That way she won't feel excluded. I need to work on a very complex case. Mother asks if you will come for lunch tomorrow?"

"Yes please."

"My mother's sister, Anna, and her husband, Trevor, will be there as usual. In the afternoon would you like to go riding?"

"I'd love to."

"We have wonderful horses – we have a riding school. You will be able to take your pick of them. The wood behind the house is brilliant to ride through when it's hot."

"I'll bring my riding gear. Thank you, darling Jason."

"Do I get a kiss?"

"Yes."

They kissed; both were filled with longing.

After lunch, as Marigold prepared to change into her riding gear, she heard Jason's father, Sir Philip (an eminent surgeon), and Lady Norton talking:

"Yes, she appears to be a very nice young woman, but we cannot have Jason mixed up with her. With her aunt's reputation, she will ruin his career. He will be a Queen's Counsel."

Marigold stood frozen. She then went outside. Jason came up to her.

"There you are!" He saw how white she was. "Are you not well, Marigold?"

"I have a headache. May I go home, please?"

"Let me take you to my mother. She will make you comfortable and give you tablets."

"Thank you – I prefer to go to my aunt."

Jason's mother, Susan, and all the family came to say goodbye. They could see Marigold was upset. She was silent on the way home.

"Do you often have headaches, darling?"

"This is my first."

He pulled into a lay-by.

"So something has upset you. Please tell me the truth, darling."

"Yes, Jason, I heard your parents talking: they think I'm unsuitable for you as I and my aunt will ruin your career."

"Oh, Marigold, I am so sorry; they are such snobs. Please, please don't let them spoil what we have. It's you I'm enjoying being with; you have given me purpose in my life. Apart from my work, I have been drifting along feeling lonely, having flings."

"I am sorry, darling Jason; I cannot continue, knowing what they think. They are right: my aunt has a terrible reputation. I only found out recently. I need to get away from her, but I will not have

9

anyone denigrating her. In her way she has been good to me."

Jason pleaded, "Forget what they said. I'll rebuke them."

"I must go."

"I will be in touch," he promised.

When Marigold got home, thankfully her aunt was on her own. Yvonne was surprised she had come home so early when she was supposed to be riding. Marigold burst out crying.

Yvonne was astounded. "Whatever has happened, darling? Has Jason come on to you?"

"No," sobbed Marigold, "our friendship is over. I would like to go to Cornwall for a while."

"Of course, darling. I'll ring Nanny. Are you driving?"

"No, I'll go by train. Have you the times, Tante?"

"I'll get them for you. When are you going?"

"This afternoon, if you don't mind."

"Why not fly?"

"I can do some designing whilst I am travelling – there's no problem changing at Plymouth. I only need take the minimum of clothing. They are such snobs, Tante."

Yvonne realised they must have been discussing her and her lifestyle.

"Have a holiday, darling, before you start work."

"I'll take my design work with me." She hugged Tante and told her she loved her, and she thanked her for caring for her since her parents died.

When Jason returned home he berated his parents, saying, "I have never been as happy as I am with Marigold. I wanted our friendship to grow; she is a treasure. She is so much nicer than the empty-headed, boring girls you have thrown at me. She has only just found out about her aunt's affairs because she has been away being educated, and has spent her holidays either in Cornwall with her nanny or in France. Marigold's parents and paternal grandparents died with her older sister and younger twin brothers in an accident when she was only eight years old, and her aunt has looked after her ever since."

Jason's parents were deeply sorry and ashamed.

"May I send her flowers and a letter saying we hope her

headache is better and that we are looking forward to her coming back and riding?" Susan asked.

Jason said sternly, "You can try, but I'm moving out. I don't want to have anything more to do with either of you."

Susan burst out crying. "Please don't say that, Jason. We adore you."

His father was also very upset.

Jason left them.

Trevor advised them, "Leave him to me." He caught up with Jason. "Please try to understand, Jason, they only want the best for you."

"The best for me is Marigold, Trevor."

"I understand. Please don't move out; it would break their hearts. Go and have a walk with Marigold and Nelson."

"Marigold has ditched me."

"Oh!"

Trevor went back to Jason's parents. They all looked worried.

"Jason is very upset. Marigold has broken with him. He really loves her."

Susan asked, "What can we do?"

"All we can do is leave it with Jason. I think I have persuaded him not to move out."

They looked relieved at that.

Jason thought his best strategy would be to leave Marigold alone for a little while. He was impatient. Nelson had to struggle to keep up with him walking so fast. Later that afternoon he rang her mobile. It was switched off. He rang Yvonne, who haughtily told him, "Marigold has gone away for a holiday."

"Has she gone to Cornwall?"

"I'm not allowed to say," and rang off.

"I feel awful," Philip said. She is a very nice young woman."

"Quite!" Trevor said sternly. "However, it's no good our sitting here feeling guilty. Let's have a walk in the wood."

They didn't meet Jason as they hoped.

Yvonne was also repentant, realising that through the selfishness and loneliness that led to her having affairs she had spoilt Marigold's chance of happiness with Jason.

Jason didn't come home for dinner, but thankfully they heard his car at just after 11. He didn't come to say goodnight.

Jason had a difficult case on, but he worked night and day, determined to go to Cornwall at the weekend. He booked in at the Rock Hotel. He knew where to find her.

Maisie was waiting at her door for Marigold. The taxi pulled up, and the driver got her bag and equipment out and carried them to the door. She paid and thanked him. She ran to Maisie, who put her arms round her. Marigold was sobbing.

"Come in, precious." Maisie waited until the storm of weeping was over. "There, there, darling! Whatever is wrong? Are you pregnant?"

Marigold had to laugh. "No, dearest Nanny, I'm still a virgin."

Maisie gave a sigh of relief. "Sit down. I'll make us a pot of tea and you can tell me if you want to."

Marigold went up to the bathroom and freshened up. Then she came back down and sat at the kitchen table while Maisie poured tea into her favourite cup. They drank in silence.

"Why did I have to grow up, Nanny? When I was a young girl I had no problems apart from my family being killed."

"Now, Marigold, this is silly talk." Maisie was always so down to earth. "You are twenty-three years old and a young lady, and you have completed a very expensive education. You are in the big wide world – especially living in London. You now have responsibilities."

"Yes, Nanny."

Marigold was beginning to feel slightly better being here. Maisie fetched her cake tin and cut her a slice of cake. Marigold ate it hungrily.

"I have your favourite pie cooking."

"Oh, thank you, Nanny. I am starving."

"Well, that's a good sign anyway," she laughed. "What your aunt told me, and the way she said it, made me think you must be suicidal and would probably starve yourself to death here." Her eyes twinkled at Marigold.

Marigold jumped up and put her arms round her. "I do love you, Nanny. I am feeling a little better now – perhaps I have been childish."

"Most likely, but human nature is what it is. Are you ready for the pie?"

"Yes please, Nanny."

Maisie gave her a good plateful and served herself. Marigold ate it as though she hadn't eaten for months. Maisie gave her another piece and Marigold told her exactly what had happened.

"Yes, I understand, but Jason didn't agree with them and he is the one who is important. It's him you say you are in love with, not his family."

Marigold began to feel foolish. Perhaps she had been hasty with Jason. She remembered the happy times they had shared, and how he helped her to get the apartment. Also, he had been polite to Yvonne.

"Perhaps I ought to ring him."

"I think you ought to leave the poor soul alone for a while. Don't make him think you are neurotic."

"Neurotic?" Marigold despite herself had to laugh.

"Best thing for you, young lady, is to have a good walk; blow your cobwebs away and let good sense in. Don't do anything hasty.

He is a thirty-two-year-old barrister and if he loves you, hopefully he will understand you have had your feelings hurt. You have come here for a holiday – use this time. Do you want to continue with him? Is he the right man for you? You have only just finished your posh school in Paris; for goodness' sake, didn't they teach you how to cope with emotions?"

"Oh no, there was nothing like that, Nanny."

"Hmm, well, get off with you, but don't drown yourself. I suppose you will be starving again in two hours."

Marigold went on to the beach and slipped her shoes off and paddled. She realised she shouldn't have run away. How childish is that! Oh well, she was here now and the apartment would soon be hers. It was time to grow up, as Maisie said. She prayed for Jason. She was filled with longing for him. She wanted to hold him in her arms and kiss him. She began weeping again. The beach was almost deserted at this time; it was late for young children to be out.

She put her shoes on and walked, deep in thought. In that time she put her childhood behind her. As Nanny had said, she was a young woman now with responsibilities. She went back to Maisie.

Maisie recognised that Marigold had been fighting with herself and had matured.

She grunted. "Freshen up, sweetheart; I have made some sandwiches and the scones you like."

Marigold hugged her. "I love you, Nanny," she said.

"Get away with you! It's not me you should be saying that to. Let's hope he doesn't meet the love of his life this week."

Marigold ran upstairs and freshened up, then ran back down for the sandwiches and scones!

When she had demolished these, Maisie made her a beaker of cocoa. She fell asleep drinking it.

"Come on, sweetheart – up we go."

Maisie helped her undress, and as she tucked her into bed she was already sound asleep.

Maisie went down and rang Yvonne again. She was out this time, but she left a message: "Marigold has eaten well and is now sound asleep. Leave her to me; let her come to her senses."

When Marigold woke up next morning, for a few seconds she wondered where was. Then she remembered what had happened and why she was there. She wanted to hide under the sheet, but she jumped out of bed, had a bath, put on shorts and a top and ran downstairs to Maisie, who was cooking breakfast. She tucked in.

Maisie told her, "You will put weight on if you are not careful."

Marigold laughed. "Oh, Nanny, a fat fashion designer! You know I have always eaten a lot and I was skinny when young."

"You were – all long legs!"

"I've still got them."

"So I see! Should you be wearing shorts as short as those?"

Marigold asked, "Do they look unladylike?"

"Don't ask me. All I am saying is that they are short – have you grown recently?"

After breakfast Marigold changed the shorts for trousers. "Will I do now?" she asked.

"Yes, you have a lovely-shaped bottom now."

"May I help you with anything, Nanny?"

"Yes, take your pad and whatever, and go and do some work to show me."

Marigold kissed her. "May I trim and wash your hair this afternoon, Nanny?" she asked.

"I suppose so, thank you."

Marigold adored Maisie.

When Marigold had gone, Maisie went to the shops and bought plenty of food. Her thoughts turned back to Marigold: she had been in London with Yvonne, and soon she would be on her own in her new apartment. She didn't know people yet, but Maisie was sure that when she began working in the shop she would meet others and make friends. She then once more thought about Jason: he would be at work and he would probably be glad to be rid of a girl who ran away instead of facing up to the situation. Maisie sighed. "Oh well, life has to be lived."

When Marigold came back at lunchtime Maisie had a good meal ready for her.

The designs Marigold had created looked good, and Maisie liked the patterns for the materials. Marigold's education wasn't being wasted.

After they had washed up, Marigold cut and shampooed Maisie's beautiful black hair. They sat out in the garden for it to dry whilst Marigold brushed it. It fell in beautiful waves.

Maisie asked her, "What are you doing this evening? I'm going to the cinema with three of my friends. Would you like to come with me?"

"I will stay here, please, Nanny. Is this OK with you? This holiday I want to do as much designing as possible before I begin work."

She was secretly hoping Jason would ring her.

He didn't; neither did her aunt. She put her heart into capturing the colours of the sky and surroundings.

Marigold worked at her designs all morning on the beach; she had made an appointment to have her hair cut in the afternoon.

She asked for a new style, and the hairdresser studied her lovely bone structure and worked round that.

Marigold was pleased; her eyes looked even bigger than ever. She thought, 'I hope Jason likes it.' Then she remembered that she might never see him again.

She also had arranged to have a manicure.

15

Marigold spent the mornings on the beach working and the afternoons with Maisie in her garden. One day they both went into town and bought materials to make Maisie two dresses from the one she had unpicked for her. She soon made one on Maisie's treadle sewing machine. Maisie was overjoyed when she tried it on; it fitted perfectly and felt so comfortable.

Marigold got on with the second one. She put the dress pieces together in her bag upstairs to take back to London with her. She had bought some off-cuts of material to make Maisie a couple of aprons of the kind she liked to wear whilst cooking. Marigold put pockets on in a plain material to give contrast.

Saturday arrived. Neither Jason nor Yvonne had rung; Marigold didn't know Maisie had advised Yvonne not to ring her.

She rang the estate agent. Her apartment would be ready for her to move into on Tuesday. She told the estate agent she was on holiday until next weekend; she gave him Maisie's number in case he needed to contact her. He thanked her.

Chapter 2

On Sunday Maisie prepared for church. She invited Marigold to go with her, but she wanted to work.

"Fair enough!" she said as she put a piece of beef into the oven to cook.

Marigold was restless. She walked to the next bay and sat between two small rocks. She had just started to copy the colour of the sky when someone nearly fell over her. It was Jason.

She rubbed her eyes.

"There you are!" he said.

"Yes – what are you doing here?"

"What do you think I'm doing here? Searching for you."

"Are you on holiday?"

"No, I'm in court early tomorrow morning. May I sit down?"

"Of course you may, Jason. You don't have to ask." She looked at him; he looked tired and strained. "Have you been working hard?"

"Yes, I'm on a very difficult case. I couldn't get away before. It was after 10 p.m. before I managed to get here. I am staying at the Rock Hotel."

They gazed at each other. Marigold began to cry. He gathered her on to his lap and held her, smoothing her hair. He gave her his handkerchief and she blew her nose. She kissed him.

"I am so sorry, Jason. I was so immature, running away from you."

"Oh well," he said, "you are in my arms now, honey. It's been one hell of a week! Are you coming back with me today?"

"Tante isn't expecting me; she hasn't rung once, and I can't just drop in on her."

17

Jason understood that she most probably had a man with her.

"My apartment is ready for me to move in on Tuesday. I told the estate agent I will be on holiday until next weekend. I need to get furniture and other things. Nanny is also expecting me to stay. I'm preparing a lot of designs and patterns ready for when I start work."

"Will you come back with me next weekend, honey?" (Her hair was the colour of honey.)

"I will, please, darling Jason. I have been so miserable."

"I've been worse. Let's walk, darling – my legs have gone to sleep!"

He helped her gather her pieces up and, carrying them for her, they walked hand in hand. They were both filled to overflowing with love.

"I have hired a car; will you and Miss Barber come for a run and afternoon tea before I have to go back?"

"Speaking for Nanny, we would love to. Have you booked your lunch at the Rock Hotel?"

"No, I would have continued searching until I found you."

She stopped walking. "Oh, darling!" she sighed. Then she kissed him passionately. She didn't care who was looking. "Will you lunch with Nanny and me?"

"I would love to, if that is OK with Miss Barber."

"It will be, sweetheart. She put a big piece of meat in the oven before she went to church."

"I looked in the church in case you were there." He laughed. "I hope I didn't disturb them too much."

She kissed him again.

"Mum and Dad are so sorry, Marigold."

She put her arm round him, and he put his arm round her waist.

"I love your new hairstyle," he said.

"Thank you. I have filled the week in the best way I could. I work every morning; then in the afternoons I spend time with Nanny. I have made her two dresses; she has one of them on this morning. I made her a couple of aprons of the type she likes to wear whilst cooking. She has been cooking for me all week, Jason. I have had an enormous appetite. I usually eat a lot, as you know, but I will be putting weight on."

He squeezed her waist. "You haven't yet, honey," he said.

"I have been pining for you, sweetheart."

"Have you really been pining for me, darling?"

"Yes, I have longed to see you, hold you in my arms and kiss you."

"So have I longed for you, honey darling."

They held each other tighter.

"When I come down next weekend, will you have dinner with me at the Rock Hotel?"

"I would love to. I will need to make a new dress; will it need to be long?"

"No, just to there." He bent down and touched her calf. "Low at the front," he teased.

"You are cheeky, Jason Norton. What colour material?"

"Gold flecks to match your beautiful eyes."

They walked on in silence. Marigold was thanking God.

When they reached Maisie's, a delicious smell of cooking greeted them.

Marigold called out, "Jason is here, Nanny."

"Yes, I thought it must be him looking in at the church. Come in, Mr Norton – you are most welcome. Are you staying for lunch?"

"Yes please, Miss Barber."

"Show Mr Norton where the bathroom is, Marigold."

They went up; Marigold ran back down.

"Well, I must say you look better. That poor man looks worn out. Will he have a beer?"

I'm positive he will, Nanny. Can I help you?"

"Set the dining table."

"Let's eat in here, Nanny, please."

"A gentleman like him will not want to eat in the kitchen."

Jason appeared.

"Yes I will, please, Miss Barber."

"Right, sir. Marigold, where are your manners? That posh Paris school must have knocked your brains out. Would you like a beer, Mr Norton?"

"Yes please." He winked at Marigold.

When she had set the table, she sat on Jason's knee. They held one another close. They were so happy and relieved. So was Maisie.

"Perhaps now she will stop eating me out of house and harbour, as they say," Maisie said.

They all laughed with joy.

"You had better ring your aunt."

"In a minute, Nanny," Marigold pleaded. "Jason would like to take us for a countryside run, and we will have afternoon tea together before he has to fly back, Nanny."

"Do you have to go back today, sir?"

"Yes. I have to be in court early tomorrow morning. It is a very difficult case, Miss Barber."

"Jason is coming back next weekend, Nanny, and I will go back with him on the Sunday afternoon. He is taking me for dinner at the Rock Hotel on Saturday evening."

"That's all right, then," Maisie said.

They all laughed.

"You don't want me with you this afternoon, Mr Norton."

"I do, please, Miss Barber."

"Then, thank you, sir. Come on – tuck in! There's plenty."

The beef was succulent; the Yorkshire puddings were perfect. Maisie had made them since her Yorkshire childhood; the vegetables and gravy were so tasty. Jason ate his plateful as though he was starving. Maisie didn't ask – she just gave them a second helping of everything. When they had eaten this, she brought out her apple pie and Cornish ice cream. They helped her wash up and then got ready for their run out.

Jason said, "What a lovely dress, Miss Barber!"

She blushed. "Marigold made it – and the one this morning. I love them. She is clever."

"We will have to go back into town, Nanny; I need to make a dress for Saturday evening. I only brought the minimum of clothing, Jason."

Jason treated Maisie with the greatest courtesy. He asked her about her life there. She told him about her friends and the church activities.

Marigold's heart went out to him. She squeezed his knee.

He murmured, "Mmm!"

Maisie sat back in the back of the car thinking, 'They had better get married soon.' She silently thanked God for answering her prayers. A pang went through her. She hadn't married. She had had boyfriends and later men friends, but she was still a virgin. So her love and maternal instincts had been showered on other young children and then the Carlisle family. She laughed to herself. Perhaps it wasn't too late to meet someone – and at least she was a good cook!

Whilst they were in the countryside, Jason asked, "Would you both like to see Hounscliffe – my childhood holiday home?"

They said they would.

When the house came into view they saw a sign: 'FOR SALE BY AUCTION'. Jason silently decided to buy it; he mentally made a note of the auctioneer's name.

He told them, "My parents sold it. My father was so busy with his work that they didn't get down here very often. My twin brothers were at boarding school and liked to holiday with their friends playing sports. When I could get away from studying, my male colleagues and I went walking in the Pyrénées."

During their afternoon tea at the Rock Hotel, Jason treated Maisie with the greatest charm; Marigold's heart ached. Jason took them back.

Later Marigold went to the car with him. He held her and they kissed passionately. He had to tear himself away. He was breathing hard.

"It's going to be another long week," he said.

"Drive carefully, darling, in the week and coming down. Are you sure you wouldn't rather fly or come on the train? You only have to change at Plymouth."

"I will be careful, honey. I have everything to live for now." Drawing her close, he kissed her again.

"I must go, honey, or I'll miss the flight," he said.

She watched him waving until he was out of sight, then she ran back in to Maisie and hugged and kissed her.

"Well, Miss, you can thank God. A gorgeous man like that – he could have any girl!"

"Yes, I know, Nanny, but he is in love with me. I'm going to be his wife."

"Has he asked you?"

"Not yet, but he will," Marigold stated with dignity.

"Well, I wouldn't be surprised if he asks you on Saturday evening. Will you be coming back here to sleep?"

Marigold was shocked. "Of course I will, darling Nanny!"

Jason instructed his solicitors to buy Hounscliffe discreetly at auction. He didn't tell his family; they had interfered with his life enough.

Marigold wanted to look her very best for Saturday evening. She made an appointment at the hair-and-beauty shop for her hair, a manicure, a facial and a leg wax early on Saturday morning.

She and Maisie went into town. She was frustrated that she couldn't find the material she had set her mind on, which Jason had asked her to match with her eyes. She hadn't her mannequin and she hadn't brought a dress she could unpick.

"Right, Nanny, I will try to find a ready-made dress. Are you tired, darling?"

"No. Carry on; I know this is important to you. If we can't find one here, we will go into the next town." Maisie remembered, "There is a dress shop up here."

When they reached it, Marigold saw *it*. It was on its own in the window, and it was exactly what she had visualised. They went in. Marigold was trembling slightly, praying it would fit her.

She asked the assistant, "Is it size 8?"

"Yes."

"Is it a one-off?"

"Of course it is," she answered snootily.

"Please let me see it." Marigold invited Maisie to sit down.

The assistant brought it to her.

Marigold examined it. "I'll try it," she said. It was too big on the bust and the sides. Marigold asked, "Are you sure it's size 8?"

"Yes."

It would be her first adult dress; she had always bought or made culottes, trousers and skirts.

"Have you anything else in the same colours?"

"No."

"I could alter it to fit, but I haven't brought my mannequin."

An older assistant came from the back.

"Are you having problems, Miss—?"

"Carlisle," she told her.

"I recognise that name. Are you in the fashion business, Miss Carlisle?"

"I will be after next week. I'm going to work in my aunt's shop as a designer."

"Has your aunt a shop, 'Yvonne', in North London?"

"Yes."

"Was your mother Koki?"

"Yes, she was."

"I remember her. What a tragedy for you – especially when you were so young!"

"Yes, Miss Barber was my nanny; she and my aunt cared for me. I'm on holiday with Miss Barber. I left London hastily, and now I am desperate for a dress for Saturday evening. I can't find suitable-coloured fabric, but this dress is perfect, apart from being too big."

"Are you able to alter it?"

"No problem."

"Would you like me to pin it for you?"

"Yes, please."

"Are you all right, Nanny?"

"Yes, precious."

Mrs Haslam asked, "Would you like a drink?"

They both said, "Yes please."

She asked the snooty assistant to make them a pot of tea. She quickly pinned the dress and helped it over Marigold's head.

"If only I had my mannequin!" Marigold said.

"I am sorry we haven't one, but you may get one at Betty's further up this road."

Marigold thanked her and they drank their tea. Mrs Haslam asked Marigold about her designing. She paid for the dress and they left.

They reached Betty's – a haberdashery, wool and textile shop. A young lady came to serve them. Maisie sat down.

Marigold asked, "Have you a size-8 mannequin for sale?"

"I believe so."

The lady went into the back and brought out a dusty one; she then took it out to the back and brushed it down.

Marigold asked to borrow a tape measure. Yes, it was her size.

"How much is it, please?"

The lady told her.

Marigold put her dress over it and then carefully took it off again.

"May I look around?"

"Please do. My name is Betty."

Maisie gave her their names.

Marigold came across some rolls of lovely materials she would be able to use. "Have you any size-8 dress patterns?" she asked.

"We should have."

She brought a cardboard box full of patterns.

They looked through and found three. They were a bit old, but lovely. Marigold knew she would need dresses if she was going to socialise with Jason. She bought the cotton and pins for her new dress as well as the rolls of fabric. Maisie bought some wool and a pattern to knit Marigold a bolero.

She asked, "How are you going to get the rolls to London?"

"Jason is driving down."

"Would you like a drink?" Betty asked.

Maisie replied, "I would, please. May I use your toilet?"

Betty showed her where it was. Then she made a pot of tea. Marigold sat down. Betty didn't want them to leave.

After chatting with her, Marigold said, "We need a taxi now. I came down on the train. I'm holidaying with Miss Barber."

"Where do you live, Miss Barber?"

She told her.

"I may be able to help you with your shopping, Miss Carlisle. Mr Nash next door lives in your area. May I go and ask him?"

"Thank you."

When she had gone, Marigold said, "We could get a taxi."

Mr Nash came back with Betty. He and Maisie had met.

"It will be a pleasure for me to bring your shopping, Miss Carlisle," he said. "I will be with you just before 6."

They thanked him and Betty.

"Please come again," Betty asked.

Maisie promised she and her friends would come to buy patterns and wool. Marigold promised her she certainly would when she was in the area.

On their way to the bus stop they went into the dress shop, Potter's, again. Marigold thanked them, and she told them she now had a mannequin; it was being delivered. The first assistant smiled at them.

They had a happy bus ride home with neighbours of Maisie.

Mr Nash brought all their shopping. He wouldn't accept anything; he said it was a pleasure to help. Marigold's fingers were itching to alter the dress.

On Tuesday Marigold received a letter from Jason's mother, saying:

We trust you are enjoying your holiday, and that Miss Barber is well.

I am sorry I hadn't the opportunity of spending time with you on the Sunday when your headache forced an early return home.

I hope you and your aunt will come for dinner one evening when you return from your holiday.

Enjoy this beautiful weather, Marigold.

Very best wishes,

Susan

Marigold replied:

Thank you for your letter and invitation to dinner. Tante and I will be very pleased to come. Miss Barber is well.

Yes, the weather is glorious. I am working hard on my colours and designs.

Marigold

On Saturday evening, when she was ready, Maisie told her, "You look beautiful, Marigold."

Marigold thanked her. "Jason is here," she said excitedly.

She went to the door, and he put the car roof up so her hairstyle wouldn't be spoiled. He looked wonderful in an obviously hand-made suit of fine pale-grey material and hand-made grey shoes. He wore a black shirt, left open at the neck.

He came in and greeted them. He told her, "You look beautiful, honey – glamorous. Doesn't she, Miss Barber?"

Maisie agreed, "She's very different from the skinny miss with long legs she was. She has filled out nicely."

Marigold blushed.

"Very nicely! Give us a whirl," Jason asked.

"You look gorgeous too, Jason," Marigold told him.

He gave her a box. Inside was a beautiful necklace and drop earrings to match the colours of the dress.

Marigold kissed and thanked him. "How did you know the colours, darling?"

"You said you would match your eyes. May I?"

He fastened the necklace and Marigold put the earrings through.

Maisie said, "That completes it."

25

Jason then gave Maisie a box. Inside was a beautiful necklace to match the two dresses Marigold had made for her. "Thank you very much, sir," Maisie said. She was close to tears. "Go on with you and enjoy your meal. I hope they have cooked plenty for you two!"

They laughed.

"I will bring Marigold home early," Jason promised.

She thanked him.

Jason helped Marigold to get into the car very carefully without creasing her dress. She had a moment's thought: 'He is practised at this.' But he had only just met her, and she was the one he was going to marry – at least, she prayed so.

She and Jason had a wonderful dinner at the Rock Hotel. This was the first time she had eaten on her own with a man in a hotel.

He told her, "You look beautiful; your dress brings out the wonderful golden flecks in your eyes. I love your new hairstyle."

"Jason, you look magnificent."

He did. He wore his obviously expensive clothes with the ease of good breeding.

He did propose during the meal and she accepted with joy.

Jason was so loving and caring. He told her about the difficult case he was working on; he had never had anyone listen so carefully. He had to restrain himself from pulling her on to his knee. He asked her about her university days and what she studied apart from design and art.

She told him, "Business studies and music."

"What else, apart from being taught how to be a proper young lady?" he teased.

Marigold laughed. "I'm a cordon-bleu cook."

"Wow! Will you cook me a meal sometime in your apartment?"

She teased him: "I will have to consider that. I would probably be so nervous that I would burn everything."

He reassured her: "I would still eat it, Marigold."

Nearing the end of the meal, she whispered to him, "I wish we were married now."

He whispered back, "So do I, honey. We needn't wait too long, need we? I don't think I can last out for very long."

She blushed.

He laughed.

After holding and kissing her, he tore himself away and returned her to Maisie.

Next morning after walking on the beach they returned to Maisie, who had cooked lunch for them again.

Marigold travelled back to London with him. He told her he had brought his car to carry her drawing equipment.

She laughed. "Darling, I brought the minimum."

"I know, but I also wanted to have this time alone with you, honey."

They talked, teased each other, and conversed in French, competing for the best pronunciation. Neither of them had ever known such happiness. Marigold told Jason his mother had written inviting her aunt and herself for dinner.

"My family are snobs, Marigold, but underneath they are very compassionate and nice. They need you to show them how to loosen up."

She asked, "What do you mean, loosen up?"

He replied, "You look at people through uncritical eyes. You have a wonderful gift of discerning the best qualities in people. You are full of joy and you are not materialistic. These are only some of your virtues, Marigold. They will learn so much from you."

She was silent.

They called at a hotel for afternoon tea and a stroll in the grounds.

Marigold asked, "Would you like me to drive?"

"If that's what you want to do, darling, thank you. I'll direct you."

He sat beside her, relaxed. He could see she was a competent and careful driver. She explained that she had gained confidence after driving on the complex road system in Paris. They had a smooth, unhurried drive back on the motorway.

"Are you able to spare me some time this evening, or do you have to stay with your aunt?"

Marigold pulled into a lay-by and rang Yvonne. "We are nearly home, darling Tante," she said. "Are you expecting me to stay with you this evening? It is such a beautiful day, I wondered if I might go for a walk with Jason and Nelson and have dinner out. Thank you, darling Tante. I will not be late back. Love you."

She turned to Jason. "Yvonne will stay longer at the shop. They have run into a problem with one of the models. May I treat you to dinner?"

"Thank you; shall I try to book a table at our pub?"

She nodded.

He rang. "Thank you. We will be with you at 8. Miss Carlisle. There – that's booked. Good! When are you moving into your apartment?"

"I will buy carpets and furniture tomorrow; I have my mummy's French cooking pans and utensils. They are stored in Yvonne's spare room along with other items."

He teased, "Will these be burn-proof?"

She laughed.

He said, "I can't wait."

Marigold then asked him, "What are your favourite foods?"

"I will eat anything you cook. I love Italian. Have you ever cooked liver?"

She promised, "I will look in my recipes."

They then spoke in Italian.

The newspapers and gossip magazines carried photographs of Jason and Marigold walking hand in hand on the beach, taking Maisie out and going into the Rock Hotel.

'Her aunt is the infamous French Yvonne dress-shop owner. Like aunt, like niece!' ran one of the articles.

Jason rang his solicitors to ask them to issue a denial: 'Mr Norton stayed at the Rock Hotel. Miss Carlisle dined with him then returned to her ex-nanny. Any insinuations of impropriety will be dealt with very severely.'

When Betty saw the photograph of Jason, she nearly swooned.

Mrs Haslam said to Peggy, "This is why she was so keen to get her dress right. I wonder why she didn't bring one with her."

"Perhaps she had run away from him."

"I wouldn't think any girl would run away from him."

Marigold read the newspapers. When she met Jason she said they needed to cool it. She said she was dragging his career and family down.

Jason pleaded, "Please don't say that, Marigold. Life without you would not be worth living. It's just paper talk. You must know how they work. Ignore them, sweetheart, to please me."

She asked, "Have you had lovers?"

"Yes, I have, darling, but no one serious. I have sown my wild oats and I am thirty-two years old, but since meeting you I haven't looked at another woman."

"Have you taken other girls to the Rock Hotel?"

"Yes, I have to tell you the truth: twice."

"So that's why people were looking at me strangely."

Jason swore. "The important thing is we haven't slept together; no one can say that. I know you are a virgin."

"Are you going out with me for sex?"

"No, darling, I am not. I admit I would like to sleep with you, but I respect you too much to even hint. Your aunt has stopped having affairs; it's a new start for all of us. Please, please, don't let anyone spoil what we have; I have never been so happy and contented since I met you. You are progressing with your work; I'm hoping to be a Queen's Counsel. I want you to be proud of me."

"I am proud of you; you are a wonderful man, darling Jason."

"Good!" Jason said with relief. "May we continue with our growing relationship? I need to warn you that the photographers will be following us to make a story. But when they see me coming to your apartment and not staying overnight, they will soon move on to their next victims."

They kissed. Jason pulled away breathing deeply.

Marigold and her aunt went to a well-known store and arranged for carpets and curtains to be fitted. They ordered everything Marigold needed for setting up home. Jason asked her not to buy a coffee-maker. He and Marigold were both good-humoured but firm with the reporters.

Jason fetched Marigold and Yvonne for dinner at his home. They both looked gorgeous; Jason told them so. Marigold wore one of her designs: pale-blue silk with tiny pansies scattered all over, a rounded neckline with long sleeves made of chiffon, and pale-blue shoes with 4-inch heels. Susan and Anna told her how beautiful she looked. They also told Yvonne the same. She wore the beautiful black dress Marigold had also created. They asked them to call them by their first names.

As they were eating, Susan and Anna asked Marigold if she could possibly spare time to design them a new outfit for Goodwood races.

"When is it?" she asked.

"End of July."

"Yes, we can always bring in extra expert dressmakers." Marigold studied their colouring; they were both tall and slim. "I suggest pale mauve for you, Susan, to set off your beautiful hair; greens will go well with Anna's colouring.

Yvonne agreed, and Marigold promised to let them see several designs; the materials would be chosen after they had approved these. She then suggested they each had a hat made co-ordinating the colours, and wore shoes and gloves dyed to match.

"Have you a mannequin?" she then asked them.

Sir Philip asked, amazed, "A mannequin?"

They all laughed.

"Darling," Susan told him, "a model of my figure to save time in the fittings."

"Oh, right! I can see Trevor and I are going to get our chequebooks out!"

"Yes," she teased him, "this is only the beginning. When Marigold has time, Anna and I need a complete new wardrobe."

They all laughed.

Jason squeezed Marigold's knee; he was so proud of her.

Anna included Yvonne in the conversation, asking her how the October show was progressing and what London stage shows she had seen.

Susan asked her the proper pronunciation of a wine they were drinking.

Yvonne pronounced it and told them, "Marigold is fluent in six languages."

Jason broke in, "Italian, and we converse in French – that's as far as we have progressed yet."

Marigold said, "I have an advantage as my mother was French."

Yvonne told them, "She was Koki, a most famous fashion designer. She was so gifted. A drunken driver killed her, Marigold's father, her paternal grandparents, her elder sister and younger twin brothers outright. There was no way Colin could have avoided him. Marigold would have been with them, but she had measles so was at home with her nanny."

Marigold looked upset; Jason put his arm round her. They all said how sorry they were.

Marigold said, "Tante took Nanny and me in; then when I went to boarding school Nanny went to Cornwall. Her parents had left her a home. I spent all my holidays with her, or my maternal grandparents in France."

Yvonne then said, "Margaret was my opposite: she was a homemaker. She adored her husband and children. She would have had more children if she had lived. Although she was haute couture, she always put her family first."

"Yes, she or daddy – or both, when possible – always read us a bedtime story."

Yvonne said, "When Marigold came home from Paris I was shocked. I thought at first she was Margaret."

They asked her, "What profession was your father in?"

She told them, "He was CEO in a very highly respected firm."

They all went quiet.

Yvonne then told them, "Marigold's parents and her maternal and paternal grandparents left her very well provided for. On reaching the age of twenty-one she also received a trust fund set up by her parents. Her sister and brother's shares automatically went to her. The money was all very well invested."

Yvonne was naughtily thinking, 'That's told them: they now know Marigold is no pauper.'

"Anna and I spent our honeymoon near the Loire Valley. Do you know it?" Trevor asked. "It's wonderful walking countryside and, being flat, it suited us."

The conversation then went around the table, discussing France and where they had been. Then Sir Philip asked Marigold about her apartment and they all said they hoped she would be happy there.

"It is going to be strange for a while until I get used to being on my own. Since I was eight years old I have been in a boarding school, university, and then finishing school, surrounded by people."

"Marigold will be able to entertain her friends and concentrate on her designs whilst on her own," Yvonne mentioned.

"My mummy's French pans and cooking utensils, a bone-china tea-and-dinner service, crystal glasses, paintings and photographs of my family and our piano and other things are stored in Tante's spare room. I will love using these."

"Marigold is a wonderful pianist," Yvonne told them proudly.

Jason was bursting with pride. "I love to sing, Marigold," he said. "We have a piano here; will you play for us soon?"

"I would love to."

Trevor, a financier, then asked Marigold, "I believe you got a 1st at Cambridge in mathematics and finance?"

"Yes, I took these subjects to come into business with Tante Yvonne."

"Your parents were obviously business people, and they would have put any money into sound investments. Am I rude if I ask the company you have your money in?"

"Not at all," Marigold assured him.

"I may be able to help you find a better investment if you so wish?"

"Yes please. I am eager to make my money work safely to the best advantage."

"Whatever we organise will be in the strictest confidence. Would you like me to give you an appointment? Are you able to come to my office?"

"Yes – I have my car."

Sir Philip broke in: "You can trust Trevor and his partners, Marigold; he has been and is good at making our money work."

Jason asked, "What make of car have you, Marigold?"

She told him, "BMW 5 Series."

"Wow! May I have a ride in it soon?"

She laughed. "I'll have to think about that."

Jason proudly said, "Marigold got a 1st also for design and art; and amongst her many talents she is a cordon-bleu cook; she has promised to cook me a meal."

Marigold broke in, "I have warned Jason I will be so nervous I will probably burn everything."

They all laughed; they were at ease with one another and delighted with Marigold.

"Marigold makes wonderful healthy bread," Jason told them.

Anna asked, "In a machine?"

"You can get good machines," Marigold replied, "but I knead manually. It is wonderful if you have a problem or if you are feeling stressed. It's so relaxing."

Jason said, "I would like to have a go."

The family laughed.

Trevor suggested, "Perhaps we could all have a go – a bread-making evening!"

"After I have practised my cooking on Jason, will you all please come for dinner?"

"Thank you, we would love to."

They all looked pleased.

After coffee Jason said, "It's time for Marigold and Yvonne to go home. Marigold has an early start."

They all warmly kissed them, thanked them for coming and how they looked forward to seeing them again soon.

Trevor said (and they all agreed), "What a lovely girl she is! It's no wonder Jason loves her."

"She is an innocent young woman. She would make Jason a good wife; she obviously adores him. She must have her mother's characteristics. I don't think she will let him have all his own way, though. Did you notice how they listen to each other? What would have happened if they hadn't forgiven us for what we said? I don't think I could have lived with myself," Philip stated.

Susan agreed: "Same here!"

"I felt sorry for Yvonne this evening. We are all happily married, and Jason and Marigold hopefully soon will be. I felt a sense of loneliness in her."

"Yes," Anna said, "so did I. I have a feeling she thinks it should have been her who died instead of her sister."

Susan broke in: "She has now turned over a new leaf. We will encourage her and let people see we are including her in our family."

"Yes," said Philip, "she isn't the only one turning over a new leaf: I was delighted when you asked Marigold to design you an outfit, old girl. It's time you came out of the 50s."

"Well!" Susan was outraged. She gave him a small kick. "Why haven't you encouraged me before?"

"You always appeared to be happy, and you run a good ship; but new clothes will give both of you a new lease of life. And, knowing Marigold, everything she will make for you will be in the best taste."

"If you want me to be more with it, will you please stop calling me 'old girl'? My name is Susan – S-U-S-A-N."

33

"Yes, of course I will, old— Susan."

They all laughed.

He put his arm round her. "We are all greatly blessed, aren't we?" he said.

Trevor reflected, "Also we are greatly blessed that our relationship with Jason, Marigold and Yvonne is restored."

They all agreed with that.

Before Jason left Marigold, he asked her, "May I go shopping with you?"

She told him, "I would love that – what about Saturday?"

"Yes please."

He teased her: "Practice before we get married!"

She laughed. "The newspapers will have a field day."

"Who cares? Please don't buy a coffee machine and beans."

Marigold made Susan and Anna a beautiful neck scarf each in wonderful patterned silk; she sent these with a note thanking them all for the evening. They were absolutely delighted.

She was very popular with her colleagues, models and customers; they admired her efficiency, her willingness to learn, her freshness and intelligence. She received many invitations. She thanked them, but said she was too busy with her new job. Marigold didn't bring Jason into her conversations, but everyone knew she was spending time with him.

Chapter 3

At Goodwood Races the outfits Marigold had had made were perfect for Susan and Anna; their husbands were very pleased with their new look.

Marigold looked beautiful in her outfit and hat. A colleague of Jason's came up and asked if he might have a quick private word. Jason excused himself.

A glamorous girl sidled up to Marigold. "So you are the mouse that is Jason's latest? Be careful – you will not last. Jason is a very sexy man, I know."

Marigold braced herself. "Jason has told me he has sown his wild oats," she said.

"Oh, the mouse has claws! Believe me, darling, you will need them."

Sir Philip noticed this interchange and rushed across.

"Will you do me the honour of escorting me to the paddock?" he asked.

Marigold looked at Susan, who smiled approval. She felt the cloak of their protection folding around her. Sir Philip gave her his arm, and as they walked he introduced Marigold to his friends and acquaintances.

A lady told Philip, "We love Lady Susan's and Anna's outfits."

Philip told her, "Thank Marigold."

They asked her, "May we get in touch?"

She gave them the address of her aunt's shop. "My aunt is in Paris just now preparing for the October show," she said, "but she has excellent staff. I will gladly design for you."

When by themselves, Philip advised Marigold, "Take no notice of Clarissa. You will need to get used to jealous young women.

Please never be upset. Talk to Jason or Susan if you are really troubled. They are all stupid empty-headed girls."

She laughed. "Oh, thank you, Sir Philip."

A television reporter came with a cameraman and asked Marigold if she might have a word. Marigold looked at Sir Philip. He nodded.

The reporter, Naomi, praised Marigold for her outfit. "Have you designed it?" she asked.

"Yes, I have."

Naomi went on: "You also designed Lady Norton's and Mrs Eyre's?"

"Yes, I did."

Philip told her, "Mr Eyre and I are very grateful for Miss Carlisle's expertise."

Naomi thanked them.

Philip was quite proud to be escorting Marigold. He told her, "Our eldest son is serving in Afghanistan. The twins are at Cambridge, but, as you know, they will be coming home soon for the holidays."

Sir Philip and Marigold met up with the rest of the party. Susan was on Jason's arm; he looked at Marigold with adoration in his eyes. The press were busy taking photographs; they were also filming.

Marigold and Jason walked arm in arm.

"You had a little confrontation with Clarissa?" Jason asked.

"Yes, I informed her that you had told me you had sown your wild oats; she replied that the little mouse has sharp claws."

Jason laughed. "Well done, darling! I adore and respect you. I have never been so happy. You have also brought happiness and a fresh breeze into my family."

Philip told Susan and Anna that some of their friends wanted Marigold to design for them.

Marigold was invited back for dinner.

Jason asked, "What would you like to do first?"

"Shall we run or swim?" she asked.

"It's a bit hot for running; what about a swim? We have a pool."

He took Marigold to fetch her costume and a dress for dinner.

When he saw her in her costume, he told her again, "You are gorgeous – slim but with wonderful curves."

She blushed.

"I'm sorry, honey – I didn't mean to embarrass you. I didn't realise how slim you are."

"I work out and run. I like to keep fit. Although I have a good appetite, I am careful what I eat and I don't drink much alcohol."

"Good!" Jason asked, "What about a bikini next time?"

"You are cheeky, Jason Norton," she retorted, and she pushed his head under the water.

He had a wonderful physique: lean with powerful shoulders and well-muscled long legs. He obviously always kept fit; she was very proud of him and told him so.

"Honey, would you rather I shaved my chest?"

She laughed. "You are perfect as you are."

They kissed.

She challenged: "Race you!"

Yvonne invited Marigold to have a talk with her.

"Darling, after you have settled into your new home, I would like to stay in Paris for a while. As you know I have to keep going over now in preparation for the show. I will not go back to my old ways, I promise you, Marigold. So, shall we have a look and see what other things of yours are in the spare bedroom?"

They had a careful browse, and Marigold was thrilled to discover some of her mother's sketches; some were in the preliminary stage with swathes of materials attached. She looked through these with hands that trembled. Yvonne had forgotten about these.

Marigold suggested, "Perhaps in our October show we could have a special slot dedicated to my mum?"

Yvonne seized on that: "Go for it, darling."

There were also paintings and photographs of the family, including Marigold with her brothers and sister.

Yvonne said, "I am so sorry she isn't here; she would be so proud of you."

They both had a good cry, and then they cuddled each other.

The chauffeur brought Jason, complete with the coffee machine and Italian beans he knew she liked. She was nervous. He hugged her, then he assembled the coffee machine.

They began on the starter. Everything tasted delicious, and Jason praised each course. As they ended the meal, he looked at her with a special look. First his eyes lingered on her hair, then her eyes, mouth and breasts. He could see her nipples becoming prominent, her breasts swelling. He pulled her on to his lap, and in a husky voice he reassured her: "It's all right, sweetheart. Just let me hold you for a few minutes."

In a quiet voice Marigold asked him, "What do you expect of me, Jason?"

"A few crumbs, that's all." He laughed. "A few crumbs! That's rich, saying that after the wonderful meal. Come on – let's wash up."

Marigold reminded him, "I have a dishwasher!"

"Yes, but you still have to load and unload it and put everything away."

They decided to dispense with the dishwasher this time. She washed; he rinsed. They dried together and tidied everything away.

She asked, "Have you washed up with any other girl?"

"No, this is a first."

She was very thankful.

Jason showed her how to operate the latest-design coffee machine. The coffee was delicious.

Security rang: "The chauffeur is here, Miss Carlisle."

"I'm going to have a swim at home. Are you going to bed, darling?" Jason asked.

Marigold told him, "First I'm going to mix some bread dough for the freezer."

"Good girl! Keep plenty of your wonderful bread going. See you tomorrow, darling honey. Shall we play tennis? Thank you again for the wonderful meal and the evening."

Philip mentioned to Susan, "Jason is looking even fitter these days."

"Yes, with Marigold's cooking and baking! He is also getting plenty of exercise, with Marigold being a keep-fit girl; perhaps we should follow their example and take more exercise?"

Philip suggested, "We could play more golf!"

Preparing the final stages for the October show was hectic as usual. Designers and models came from Paris, Italy and America. It was an international production. Marigold's knowledge of languages was put to very good use.

Backstage there was the usual chaos. A broken fingernail was a major disaster to a model, but when they were on the catwalk the girls were all so professional and gorgeous. Everything up front went smoothly at least. Outfits were reserved for customers. The famous designers, models and film stars were being interviewed for television and the fashion magazines.

After a break Yvonne walked on to the catwalk and announced, "Now, here is the special nostalgic showing of the famous Koki designs that had been put away after her and her family's tragic accident. It is with the greatest honour that we now present Koki's daughter, my niece, Marigold Carlisle's completion of these designs."

The models came on, and although the styles were fourteen or fifteen years old everyone gasped at the cut and colours of these outfits. Designers were photographing every one to copy.

When the models congregated at the finish, everyone stood up out of respect for Koki and Marigold, and they clapped and cheered. It was a major success. Yvonne brought Marigold on. She was crying.

Jason rushed backstage to wait for her. He then held her in his arms. Several models were wondering who this gorgeous man was.

They all went on to a party afterwards to celebrate (a) the show being such a success and (b) all the orders received. The papers, magazines and television gave it rave reviews. They all mentioned how brave Miss Carlisle had been and thanked her for allowing these designs to be shared.

Chapter 4

Out walking on the heath with Nelson, Jason said, "Honey, now we are established I have something to tell you. I would like to buy Hounscliffe for a holiday home for our future children and us. If you don't approve, I'll not go ahead; it is to be auctioned, you remember."

Marigold pulled him close to her side.

"Darling, you are wonderful," she said. "How marvellous! I am thrilled. I love you more and more each day."

"I adore you, sweetheart. I will give the agents the go-ahead. When it is settled and we have the survey we will get the repairs done first and then sort everything else out. Do you think we will be able to go down some weekends? You could stay with Maisie and me at the Rock Hotel?" Jason asked.

"We will work round that definitely. We could go down on a Friday evening by train or fly, when we don't have to work Saturdays, and come back on the Sunday afternoon." Marigold asked, "How many rooms are there?"

Jason thought. "I remember there were ten bedrooms; eight are en suite. Downstairs there is a morning and dining room, a lounge and a big family kitchen. What will please you, darling, is that there is a bread oven in the wall Our housekeeper used to make our bread; and I remember a big Aga. We used to sit in front of it to make toast."

"Oh, I will love that if it's still in."

"If they have got rid of it, I will buy you another."

"We could get the kitchen and master bedroom ready, and then you and I could stay there for weekends, darling Jason."

"Do you mean you and me . . ."

"I do, my darling."

Jason was full of joy. "When shall we get married?" he asked. "What about early December?"

"Honeymoon at Hounscliffe?"

"Brilliant – so shall we get engaged?" Jason asked her.

"We need to tell my family and Yvonne, honey."

"Let's see if we get Hounscliffe first."

"We will get it, sweetheart."

Marigold suggested, "While we are sorting Hounscliffe out, when we marry we could live in my apartment, don't you think?"

"I would be happy to live in a tent as long as I'm with you, honey."

"What kind of home would you like?"

"When Hounscliffe is settled, we will ask the agents to make enquiries. It must be right for us and our children. How many children would you like?"

"Lots," laughed Marigold. "Jason, I have plenty of money; I would like to contribute to our family home."

"If that is what you want to do, sweetheart, you will have to tell Trevor you will need some money; thankfully I also have plenty so we will push the boat out."

"We will have to set both homes up," she teased.

"Perhaps we will have plenty of engagement and wedding presents," he came back with.

They sat down on a bench. Jason told her, "I can't believe my good fortune, knowing you are actually going to marry me. I will always adore and take care of you, darling. I will always be faithful."

Marigold teased him: "You had better be! Let's go and eat."

"I don't think I will be able to eat – I am too excited."

She teased him again: "You had better eat – you now have to build your strength up!"

Jason lightly smacked her bottom.

Marigold asked Jason, "Please take great care when you are driving, darling."

"Now, Marigold, I understand the trauma of your family's accident must still be with you; I have everything to live for now I have you, and I promise to be careful. Would you like me to use the chauffeur?"

She laughed and kissed him. "I pray God will keep us safe," she said.

The next evening Marigold and Yvonne had dinner at Jason's; they told Jason's parents about Hounscliffe. Marigold had already told her aunt that she and Jason were going to get married in early December, hoping she approved.

Yvonne had been overjoyed and wished them all happiness. "You are made for each other; you will have a wonderful life," she said.

Jason told his parents. They also were overjoyed.

Philip said, "This calls for champagne!"

The butler fetched the bottles.

Jason suggested they keep all this news to themselves for the time being. They all agreed.

"The reporters will not give you a minute's peace when word gets out," said Philip.

Susan told Marigold, "Any time you are here late, darling, you could stay overnight."

Marigold went bright red, so Susan quickly said, "I mean there are plenty of spare en-suite rooms."

Marigold and Jason laughed.

"Now, Mum, I began to think you were putting temptation in our way," said Jason.

"Oh dear! I suppose it did sound like that."

They all laughed and Marigold thanked her for her kind thought.

Jason, his family and Yvonne came to Marigold's for dinner; she had pulled all the stops out. They enjoyed each course and congratulated her. When they had completed the meal Jason pulled her on to his lap; she blushingly protested.

He held her close, saying, "What a treasure we have here!"

They all agreed.

"Jason, you have always looked fit, from working out, playing sports and walking, but we all think you look even more so lately," Trevor remarked.

"Yes, with Marigold I am exercising more. It is the only way I can get rid of my work stress. She won't let me do anything else!"

Marigold protested: "Oh, Jason!"

They all laughed.

Susan told her, "We are very proud of you. In these days it's a relief to know an innocent young lady."

Jason said, "I have the world in my arms. What else could I possibly need?"

They all agreed.

Susan quietly said, "Let's leave them. We'll start clearing away."

Jason and Marigold weren't used to this! They helped to carry everything through to the kitchen. Jason set the coffee machine going.

"Right, Marigold washes; I rinse. You five, wipe and put on the table!" Jason said.

Jason's parents were really enjoying themselves in this relaxed atmosphere. They helped Marigold and Jason to put things away, and then everyone went through to the lounge for coffee. They admired Marigold's paintings, which she told them had come from her parents' home. Security rang – the chauffeur had arrived.

They all kissed Marigold and told her they had never enjoyed an evening more. They allowed Jason a few minutes to say goodnight.

"See you tomorrow, darling." Marigold said. (They had planned to lunch at Jason's and then to ride in the wood afterwards.)

Jason's agent secured Hounscliffe for a good price.

Jason and Marigold flew to Cornwall the next Friday evening. Jason had hired a car for the weekend.

After breakfast at the Rock Hotel, he collected Marigold and they went to Hounscliffe. Maisie insisted they went on their own; she said she would have a good meal waiting for them at lunchtime.

The caretaker/gardener and his wife, Mr and Mrs Goodwin, who lived in the cottage just outside the gates, were waiting for them. Their dog, Barney, barked when they arrived. Nelson went sniffing round him.

After introductions, Mr Goodwin told them, "We are very pleased it's sold; three years is a long time for a house to be empty. We would like to stay on, sir. Please call me Alistair, and my wife Gladys, Miss, sir; Gladys is one of the cleaners and also an overseer."

Marigold and Jason welcomed this. "It will help so much, as both of us will be so busy in London."

Gladys asked, "May I bring you a hot drink up soon? The gas is on, but the electricity is still switched off."

"Yes please. May we have strong coffee?"

The estate agent, Mr Hall, was also waiting outside. After greeting them he told them the survey had revealed that certain minor repairs were needed. Otherwise the house was sound; the most serious thing was that a few tiles were missing from the roof. Alistair and Gladys had had it kept in good repair.

They all went into a roomy cloakroom leading to the very large kitchen. The range was still there, as was the bread oven. A nine-ring gas cooker stood beside the range. The floor was of Cornish slate. There was a big open fireplace and a large well-scrubbed table. It was homely and lovely, spotlessly clean. Marigold was thrilled; she fell in love with it.

The master bedroom was very large with an open fire, and the bay windows overlooked the countryside; they could see the sea in the distance.

The en-suite was also roomy. Jason suggested having a complete new suite in their colour. The other eight en-suite rooms needed updating. Each bedroom had a small fireplace and an oil-fired radiator heated from the range. Everywhere needed redecorating and new carpets.

"What about the other two bedrooms having an en-suite?" Jason asked. "If we are going to have lots of children, as you say, we will need these. We may as well set this up whilst the plumbers are here."

"That's a good idea, darling," Marigold agreed.

Gladys called upstairs: "Coffee is ready, Miss."

Marigold and Jason went down and asked her and Alistair if they would join them.

Gladys had set the table; she said, "Leave the pots, Miss. I'll come back later." She tactfully left them on their own to discuss the repairs needed.

The coffee tasted lovely. Alistair said, "It's the water here."

Nelson drank two bowlfuls of water straight off.

"Thank you, Alistair, for opening the windows every day to let the air in," Jason said.

"Will you please light the range tomorrow morning early? Miss Carlisle has brought a casserole and Miss Barber is coming for lunch."

"Of course, sir. Anything we can do, please leave a note or ring us."

"We will now pay your wages, Alistair."

44

"Thank you, sir, but Mr Grocutt has paid us up to the end of the month." (Mr Grocutt was the previous owner of Hounscliffe.)

"Call that a little bonus, Alistair."

"Much obliged, sir. Of course, when you come for your holidays, Gladys and I will only do our duties and not interfere with you."

"Thank you, Alistair." Jason asked the estate agent and Alistair, "Will you recommend a plumbing firm, decorators and carpet fitters?"

"I have this information ready, sir; I thought you would ask. If there is anything else I can help you with, please let me know," Mr Hall replied.

"When the plumbers have finished with our bathroom, Miss Carlisle and I would like the other bathrooms to be updated."

Alistair endorsed the workmen Mr Hall had recommended.

"The master bedroom en-suite is our first priority," Jason told them, "and then at least four of the other en-suites need to be made ready for our families coming for holidays later."

After their coffees, they went outside with Alistair. It looked neglected, with peeling paint, but Mr Hall reassured them: "The woodwork is still sound – no decay despite the weather, and no woodworm anywhere in the house."

Alistair verified this.

Mr Hall recommended having all the paintwork attended to as soon as possible before the winter. "Although we have mild winters, we do get plenty of rain," he said.

Marigold and Jason laughingly said they knew that.

"There are just a few slates off the roof, sir, but the chimneys and gutters are sound. The roof people are coming on Monday to attend to this; this work is covered by Mr Grocutt's insurance." Mr Hall then said, "I will leave you now, unless you need to ask me anything further? Can you get into Polzeath this afternoon to see the painters?"

They promised to be here for about 2.30.

Jason and Marigold went back upstairs and made notes of what needed replacing in the bathrooms.

Jason suggested, "We could order everything from the London store and have it delivered."

"That's a good idea, darling. This will save time."

"We'll co-ordinate the delivery with the plumbers."

Marigold laughed.

Jason put his arms round her. "What is it, honey?"

"Well, I was thinking that we have only known each other for three months!"

"I feel as though I have known you for ever, my darling honey. We are soulmates."

"Yes, we are, sweetheart. I love you."

They kissed, then Jason, breathing heavily, said, "Come on – let's go back to Miss Barber and eat the delicious lunch she will have cooked."

Nelson jumped up at that.

Mr Hall was waiting; they went to the paint stores. He had made an appointment with Geoff, who was the owner. Mr Hall introduced them.

Maisie took Nelson for a walk.

Jason explained, "Miss Carlisle and I are getting married in early December and we would like to spend our honeymoon at Hounscliffe. All the outside woodwork has been neglected, so we would like to have this prepared and painted as soon as possible."

Geoff looked in his diary. "I could start with three of my men in two weeks' time, scraping off the old paint and then treating the wood ready for the undercoat. The long-range weather forecast is good. What colour have you in mind, Miss?"

"As before – white, please."

Jason then said, "There will be all the inside then; but if you could decorate the master suite, top priority, we can have the carpet fitted."

"You'll not want us whilst you are spending your honeymoon there, sir."

Jason laughed. "Well!"

Marigold was blushing. She said, "I would like to choose the wallpapers in London to save our time. If I fax you the details, will you be able to obtain them?"

"We will do our best, Miss."

"Also, I would like to design the paper for around the fireplaces, so I can match the curtains."

"I look forward to seeing this paper, Miss. Is designing your job?"

"I am a fashion designer."

Geoff shook hands with Jason and Marigold. "Call me Geoff,"

he said. "Congratulations, Miss, sir, on your getting married. You will be warmly welcomed by the community when you spend your holidays and weekends here. Are you coming next weekend?"

"That depends on our work, Geoff. I am a busy barrister."

"Right, sir. Rest assured we will get things started down here as soon as possible."

They thanked him.

Next Mr Hall took them to the plumber's shop, and Jason outlined his requirements.

"Miss Carlisle and I are busy career people so it will be easier for us to order what we want in London and have it delivered when you are ready to install. The London store stays open until 10 three evenings a week."

The plumber welcomed this. "We haven't much space here, sir," he said.

"We will order tiles to match. Miss Carlisle and I would like the other bedrooms made en suite whilst you are there, if that is possible. Our families then will be able to come for holidays."

Tony told them, "We have three weeks' work, and then we could book you in to begin the tiling."

Jason asked, "Will you please do the master suite first? We are getting married in early December, and we are hoping to honeymoon at Hounscliffe."

"We will get on, sir, as soon as we have the tiles and the suites. You will not want us while you are on your honeymoon."

Jason and Marigold laughed.

"That's just what Geoff, the painter, said," Marigold replied.

"We can bring reliable colleagues in to help us to get it all done. We will get it all done and then cleaned up."

They shook hands.

Outside, Marigold asked, "Shall we have a cup of tea?"

They went and found Maisie and Nelson, who both looked happy.

The café staff were pleased to have them; they knew they were important by their clothes and voices. A waitress brought a white china teapot and matching crockery and made them some tasty sandwiches. Then she brought a plate of home-made scones with jam and Cornish clotted cream.

Geoff appeared in the doorway as they were enjoying their

sandwiches. "Sorry to intrude, sir, Miss. I have been looking for you."

Jason invited, "Come in, Geoff. Would you like a cup of tea?"

"A painter never refuses a drink!"

The waitress brought another cup.

"What about something to eat?" Marigold asked him.

"Thank you, Miss, but I'm going home soon. My wife will have cooked. What I have come to tell you is that a colleague of mine has just been in the shop. The job he is on has been held up for three days or so because the builders haven't finished as scheduled. Assuming this would be all right, I have set him to work, getting your old paint off and treating the wood. He is a first-class painter and may be able to help us later."

Jason thanked him.

As he left, Geoff said, "Thank you for the cuppa," and he waved to the waitresses.

They came back to the table and asked, "Would you like a fresh pot of tea?"

"Yes please. Everything is lovely. May Nelson have a drink of water, please?"

"Of course. Are you holidaying?" (The waitress had seen Maisie around.)

"No," Jason told her, "we have bought a holiday home. We are only here for the weekend."

"Are you coming down next weekend, sir?"

"It depends on our work. Miss Carlisle is a busy fashion designer and I'm a busy barrister. We usually have to work on Saturdays. Miss Carlisle is staying with Miss Barber. I am at the Rock Hotel."

"Oh, please come again."

Jason gave her his most charming smile. "We will," he said. "Miss Carlisle and I are getting married in early December; we are going to spend our honeymoon at Hounscliffe, which we have bought. It was my childhood holiday home."

Maisie enquired, "Where are the toilets, please?"

"We have only one. I will show you."

One of the waitresses brought them a fresh pot of tea, smiling at them. When Jason went to pay, he gave them a tip. Marigold and Maisie smiled at everyone and thanked them.

All the café staff came to the door and waved to them as they left. The other customers were also waving!

When they were out of earshot Marigold told him, "Well done, darling. The local people will soon see that we are friendly."

"I thought I would spoil their gossiping about us living together by telling them the truth."

"Yes, well done, Mr Norton!" added Maisie.

"Please, Miss Barber, call me Jason."

"I will if you call me Maisie."

He gave her a hug. Then he teased her: "Their scones were delicious – nearly as nice as yours, Maisie!"

She said, "Go on with you!"

They were all happy.

Jason had breakfast at the Rock Hotel. He collected Marigold and they went back to Hounscliffe to make more lists of requirements.

Alistair had the range hot for the casserole. They boiled a pan of water and made coffee. Jason fetched Maisie whilst Marigold prepared the vegetables.

Marigold designed the patterned wallpaper for around the fireplaces. The wallpaper company had the rolls manufactured and asked Marigold if they might use the designs in their latest pattern book?

She asked Jason, who said, "It's up to you, darling."

After thinking, she agreed to their using a slightly different version of her original design. They paid her a good sum for this and requested further designs.

Chapter 5

A popular early evening television chat-show producer asked Marigold if she would give them an interview about her designing outfits and hats. Marigold asked Jason, who was thrilled for her. The presenters and producer met with her a few days before recording to prepare for this. Marigold suggested they film her using her computer to match colour of hair and eyes, as well as skin tone, then mixing dyes to get the right shades for the materials of the outfits, including hats, gloves and specially dyed shoes made up by the shoemakers.

Then they filmed her at the shop and in the office where she worked. They showed her at her desk doing the financial work with a PA, making outfits and putting them on the mannequins and designing hats with the subcontractors. They then showed the completed outfits with the shoes and handbags. Marigold was shown in close discussion with Yvonne, colleagues and models.

The male presenter opened the interview by welcoming Marigold and thanking her for her time. He asked if she was enjoying her work, and she told him she loved it.

The films were shown, while Marigold explained what she was doing. She said, "This is only a part of the preparation we do for the outfits."

The presenter was amazed about the shoes; he hadn't realised the materials had to be dyed before being made.

Marigold laughed.

"Is designing in your blood?" the lady presenter asked.

"Yes, my mummy was Koki, the famous designer. She, my daddy, his parents, my elder sister and my younger twin brothers were killed in a car accident caused by a drunken driver when I was eight years old. I would have been with them, but I had measles so I was at home with my nanny."

"Your mother would be proud of you."

"I hope so."

"And then what happened?"

"Tante Yvonne took Nanny and me in. I was and am very grateful to her for her care and commitment. I went to boarding school; Nanny went to live in Cornwall. I spent all holidays from school and university either with her or with my maternal grandparents in France. For the last two years I have been in Paris at a finishing school."

"What were your subjects at Cambridge?"

"I did computer graphic art, hand art and design, and business studies."

"What grades did you achieve?"

"I was very lucky to get a 1st in all my subjects. Whilst at the finishing school I studied haute couture and cordon-bleu cooking. I love cooking – that is another of my designing skills: preparing a meal and presenting it."

The male presenter laughed. "We have been told you make marvellous, healthy bread."

"Yes," Marigold laughed. "I love to make bread. Mixing the dough with my hands is wonderful when I am feeling a little stressed when my work isn't progressing in the time I have promised to complete it. Kneading the dough is wonderful therapy – I recommend it heartily."

"Do you still live with your aunt?"

"No, I have an apartment."

"We have had numerous e-mails from young ladies and men asking if you can advise them on how they can get into the fashion business, from dressmaking to designing. Are you willing, Miss Carlisle, to give them some tips?"

"I am. There are many online contacts; I recommend these. I concentrated on mathematics in my schooldays; this greatly helped me when I took business studies at university. Also, mathematics is, amazingly, needed in all dressmaking. Begin by learning how to use a sewing machine. Cut out from patterns and pay good attention to details. We all have to begin somewhere. Accept criticism of your work and learn from this. Never forget we wouldn't be able to sell clothes if they hadn't been produced. Take pride in your work. Be artistic, creative and imaginative. You need to have normal colour vision."

The presenters thanked her.

"You have been approached by a famous chain store to design a new range for young ladies and children."

"Yes, I am excited about this. We mustn't envy the rich and famous; they bring employment for hundreds of people and help the economy. But this new work gives me more opportunity of mixing and matching. A well-cut pair of trousers or skirt can be matched with a different top or shirt to ring the changes. Young people need clothes that are quick-drying and non-iron. Cheap accessories are also vital – a belt with a modern buckle, unusual buttons, gems and rhinestones, stick-on sequin patches or a piece of jewellery can make the world of difference."

The lady presenter told her, "My daughter and her friends are greatly looking forward to your designs."

Marigold thanked her. "I was fortunate: I didn't have to worry about paying my fees and my parents left me money for my education, but I appreciate that some of our young people have to manage the best way they can."

"You are a keep-fit advocate, Miss Carlisle?"

"Yes, I love all sports."

"Mr Norton also enjoys sports with you," added the male presenter.

"This interview is about my work, not my personal friends," Marigold told him quite sternly.

"Quite! I apologise."

Marigold smilingly reassured him: "I would have asked the same question."

"We have enjoyed having you with us and giving us an insight into the fashion world. We do hope you will be able to come back soon?"

"I would love to," she said.

The cameramen and everybody else began clapping. Marigold laughed as she was given a bouquet.

When she had left, the lady presenter said, "What a pleasant young lady! I didn't want her to leave."

The male presenter agreed. "We must have her back soon," he said.

When Marigold arrived home, security gave her a bouquet from Jason with a card which read, 'See you soon. Love you.'

Yvonne was delighted with the interview and she was impressed by Marigold's expertise.

When Jason came for dinner he told her, "I am so proud of you. You were very mature, honey. Your lovely personality and intelligence shone through." He also brought his family's best wishes and congratulations.

Over the next few days Marigold received many invitations to appear on television.

Marigold had to work on the following Saturday morning to complete a hat. She had promised Jason she would help him to buy a birthday present for his mother. She had suggested one of the latest small shoulder/hand bags.

He came to pick her up. He stood outside looking at the window displays, then went in. He greeted Yvonne, kissing her hand; she introduced him to the staff and several models. Jason was enjoying himself. They were all laughing and teasing him for being in the shop. Marigold was still in her workroom. He asked if he might go through. Yvonne took him in.

Marigold saw him. He looked debonair and relaxed. His pale-grey trousers showed off his strong thighs and slim waist; his shirt showed his powerful shoulders. She was so proud of him.

"May I look around?"

She showed him her latest project, and he was amazed at how much behind-the-scenes work was involved.

Marigold showed him a handbag and suggested that a similar one could be made for his mother. He knew she would love it.

"Do you think we ought to have one made for Aunt Anna?" he asked. "It will be her birthday in a few weeks."

Marigold assured him she would arrange this.

She introduced him to her colleagues, and he had a coffee whilst Marigold tidied up.

They went and had lunch. Jason continued asking her about her work. Her heart was singing, having someone to share with.

"You are wonderful, darling. Thank you for taking an interest in my work and listening."

"I understand what you mean, honey; you listen to me talking about my work and interests too. I know from your questions that you really take in what I say. You are a treasure to me. I wake up every morning thinking I have dreamed you; then I remember you are not a dream. You have no idea how happy you have made me or how much I love you."

Marigold teased him: "I hope I never turn into a nightmare!"

He laughed. He adored her humour.

Chapter 6

In her lunchtime Marigold went looking at bathrooms in the store. She spotted Clarissa heading her way. She groaned but stood her ground.

"I would have thought your latest-design apartment had the upmarket equipment."

Marigold answered, "I'm just passing through."

Clarissa spitefully told her, "I see you are managing to hold on to Jason, but after you have slept with him he will tire. He is enjoying the chase. You are different, but, believe me, it will not last. I know him."

Marigold told her, "I hope and pray you will fall in love, Clarissa. You will not then feel lonely and vindictive."

Clarissa stormed off.

Marigold groaned, thinking she had reacted badly, but unknown to her one word had struck home: *lonely*.

Clarissa realised, 'Yes, that's it – I am lonely.' She was looking at life with hardness and jealousy. She was a millionaire through her family and without having to work, but she also realised that, although they had provided money, they hadn't given or shown her love. They had been too busy making money to give her their time. Nannies had brought her up.

She went home and walked in the grounds, thinking she hadn't any purpose in her life apart from the empty endless rounds of parties and all the cattiness. She was jealous of Marigold not just because Jason was in love with her, but also because Marigold had a purpose in her life with her work. It dawned on her that Marigold had worked hard at school and university to achieve her success. She was worse off than Clarissa in that Marigold's family had been killed when she was young, but despite this she hadn't become bitter and blamed everyone.

Clarissa began to think along different lines: 'Where am I going? Get married? That's what my family expect of me, but why would a man marry me except for my money? Who can I really talk to? Who listens? I never listen, except to malicious gossip.'

She went up to her room and watched the video of Marigold's interview. Her maid came up, and through the open door she could hear Clarissa crying. She couldn't believe it. She didn't know what to do. She knew that if she interrupted, Clarissa would bite her head off. She ran downstairs.

Clarissa's mum, Linda, was getting out of her car. She looked startled when Joanne ran up to her.

"Excuse me, ma'am. Please come. Clarissa is crying!"

"Thank you, Joanne. Leave her to me."

She ran upstairs.

"What is it, Clarissa? Are you pregnant? Is it Aids? Have you been taking drugs?"

Clarissa still sobbed.

Linda was at a loss. She rang her husband; he was playing golf.

"You must come home immediately; we have a problem with Clarissa."

He dashed home.

Clarissa was still sobbing. She was trying to talk, but the words wouldn't come.

Matthew said, "We had better get the doctor."

Clarissa shook her head. "No, no."

Linda fetched her a glass of water and sat on the bed at her side.

Matthew thought, 'This is the first time I have been in her bedroom.' He and Linda were looking at each other puzzled. They waited until Clarissa calmed down.

"What is it, Clarissa?" Linda asked her in a stern voice.

Clarissa told them, "I am not pregnant; I haven't got Aids; I am not on drugs – I have tried them, but they made me feel ill and not in control. I have no real purpose in my life; I am shallow, selfish, bitchy, jealous. Most of my friends only want me because I am your daughter and for my money."

Her parents were speechless!

Then Matthew said, "I need a drink."

Clarissa told him, "No, Daddy, that isn't the answer. Will you, *please*, for the first time in my life *listen* to me?"

He was dumfounded. She had never spoken to him like that before. In fact, she had spoken to him very little unless she needed something. At mealtimes she ignored him.

"I have been absolutely beastly to Marigold," Clarissa continued. "I have put doubts in her mind that Jason will dump her after she has given him her virginity. Her parents, grandparents, elder sister and young brothers were killed when she was a young child, but *she* has made something of her life. I am jealous."

They discussed Marigold and her interview.

"Yes," Matthew said, "she obviously isn't short of money, but her aunt can't have been much good to her."

Clarissa bitterly said, "She took her in – she didn't neglect her."

"We appreciate this talk, darling, but we have never neglected you; we have provided you with everything you needed and wanted."

"You *have* neglected me," Clarissa shouted at them. "Money isn't everything; you haven't shown me love. You haven't given me your time. You haven't read me bedtime stories. Nannies have brought me up. I feel as though I have been a nuisance in your busy, career-controlled lives."

"Now, look here," spluttered Matthew, "you haven't had to work; you have had the best education and luxuries owing to our careers, as you call it."

"You are still not listening to me, Daddy. I have been and am lonely, I haven't had any brothers or sisters because you have both been pursuing your careers. I am living an aimless life. I have got into the crowd I go about with because I feel rejected."

Linda soothed her: "I am listening now, darling. I am beginning to understand what you are saying."

Matthew muttered, "I wish I were!"

Linda gave him a black look. "What can we do?" she asked.

"Spend more time with me. Take an interest in what I am doing, and encourage me to have a worthwhile life."

"We need to spend more time together, is that it? Do you like playing golf?"

At this Clarissa laughed. "I will learn, Daddy," she said.

"Could we have a holiday together?" Linda then asked.

"Yes please."

"Right, shall we rent a villa in Portugal?"

Matthew told them, "There are plenty of good golf courses there."

They all laughed.

He thought he was dreaming – was this really his daughter?

"Shall we three go out for dinner?"

"Thank you. I am playing tennis, but I won't go on to the party afterwards."

Matthew promised, "I will fetch you home." (This was a first.) "And then shall the three of us have dinner?"

"Please don't be jealous of Marigold," Linda pleaded. "There are plenty of Jasons about. You have been with the wrong crowd, darling."

"No, that is wrong. They are like me: just drifting aimlessly."

"Shall we have a cup of tea outside?" Linda suggested.

Matthew rang the housekeeper and went down for a smoke.

Clarissa washed her face. Linda brushed Clarissa's hair; then they went down hand in hand.

"Ask any of your friends to come on holiday with us, darling," Linda said.

"No, thank you, Mummy. I would like to spend time with just you and Daddy. Do you think I should write to Marigold apologising for my behaviour?"

"That would be very mature of you, darling."

When they had had a cup of tea, Clarissa dropped a bombshell: "I would like to go to a finishing school in Paris. I want to learn to cook and further my education."

Linda was – well, she didn't know what she was, but she knew they had had a lucky escape.

Later, whilst by themselves, Matthew said to Linda, "I have actually begun to like Clarissa; I have always found her difficult and surly in the past."

Linda agreed with him: "Same here! It must be a miracle."

Matthew asked, "Is it too late for us to provide her with a brother or sister?"

Linda nearly fainted! "I wouldn't think so; let's ask Clarissa if that's what she would like."

Over dinner they asked her and she was delighted, but she asked, "Will there be any danger to you, Mummy?"

"I will make an appointment to see Malcolm" – their family doctor – "to make sure everything is in working order. I had no problem with you, darling. I am so sorry I have been too busy with my career to have more children before. Your daddy and I are sorry about a lot of things, but we are going to be different from now on. May we delay our holiday for a few days until I have the all-clear?"

"Yes, Mummy. Portugal should do the trick," she added mischievously.

"It looks like it will be a good holiday," Matthew added.

Her other friends didn't want to change their lifestyle, so Clarissa broke away from them.

Linda was given the all-clear. Everything was healthy; there should be no problem with her having a baby.

Yvonne and Lady Susan were amazed to receive a telephone call from Linda inviting them to lunch at Claridge's – Tuesday if possible; and Marigold was astounded to receive the following letter, which came to the shop delivered by hand on the following Monday morning:

I am so sorry I have been so bitchy with you, Marigold. You did not deserve this. I was jealous of your friendship with Jason and how you have made something good of your life.

After I had seen you on Saturday I was completely honest with my parents: I said that I was resentful of their neglect and their being so busy with their careers when I was growing up. However, that is all behind us now, and we are going for a holiday in Portugal together. Daddy is going to show me how to play golf!

Also, thanks to you, Marigold, three of my friends and I are going to the finishing school in Paris.

I wish you and Jason all the very best. He is a wonderful man and he deserves a good lady like you, Marigold.

Sincerely yours,

Clarissa

Marigold showed Jason the letter. He also was astounded.

"You are setting a good example, darling. You will make a wonderful wife for a judge."

"Oh," she teased, "are you dumping me and passing me on?"

He grabbed her. "You are going to be my wife, sweetheart."

Linda told Yvonne and Susan over lunch what a good influence Marigold had been in Clarissa's life and how she was changing. She told them about the previous Saturday and how repentant she and Matthew were for neglecting Clarissa. "We have resolved never to neglect her again, thanks to her being honest with us," Linda said. "We are going to Portugal together – it will be our first holiday together. And, with Clarissa's permission, Matthew and I are going to try for a brother or sister for her. I was examined yesterday, and I have been given approval to go ahead. We and the other parents are making arrangements for Clarissa and her friends to enrol at a Paris finishing school. The other friends didn't want to change their lifestyle, so Clarissa broke away from them. Matthew and I feel so proud when we tell our relatives and friends about Clarissa going to Paris and learning to cook as one of her subjects."

Yvonne and Susan were so pleased at Linda's words; they thanked her for telling them.

Susan said, "Marigold is a good influence on me, and my family's life also." She told them about how they had started kneading bread dough by hand because Marigold had told them it helped get rid of stress.

Linda laughed. "Matthew and I must have a go at this!" she said.

Yvonne revealed that Marigold had had a good influence on her life also. "There is no denying I have had affairs," she said, "but I am ashamed. My excuse also is that I was lonely and selfish. The fashion business is full of temptations, but we know Marigold has her head screwed on and she has Jason. I also am now making a new beginning, and I already feel much happier and more settled."

Marigold had arranged to come for dinner at Jason's after their swim.

Susan invited Anna and Trevor as she wanted to tell them about the lunch with Linda and what Clarissa has said. They were all delighted.

Jason pulled Marigold on to his knee and cuddled her. They were all relaxed with one another.

Out walking, Jason mentioned, "Honey, I booked a walking holiday in the Pyrénées with some of my colleagues. We have done this every year since we met at university, but I will cancel it."

"No, sweetheart, they would be disappointed. I will use this time to fill my freezer and Tante's. It will be useful for us to have some quick meals ready. I will also be able to get plenty of designing done, which will mean I should be free when you return."

"My colleagues would love to meet you properly."

"What do you suggest?"

"What about meeting up with them this Friday evening, have a walk, then dinner at our pub. They know not to intrude on our times together."

"This sounds good to me, but will they expect me to cook for them?"

"No, sweetheart, not this time."

"I will another evening, then," she promised.

When they met up, Jason introduced them. (Marigold had seen them whilst out walking or running.) They were two doctors (Christopher and Kevin), three solicitors (Kenneth, Nigel and Adrian), and a police inspector (Daniel). They liked one another on sight. They had a happy walk. Nelson was excited, having three dog friends with him. They went to the pub.

As they sat together they assured Marigold that they would take great care of Jason.

She asked, "Please do."

Daniel asked, "What will you do while Jason is away?"

She told them about the cooking and designing. "I have extra work on just now setting up the chain-store requests," she added.

"You will not have much time to get into mischief."

Nigel laughed. "So you will not feel too lonely, I am willing to stay with you. I like cooking."

They all laughed at that.

"He can't even make toast," said Kenneth.

Jason came in with, "Later on, Marigold would like to cook you a meal."

They thanked her and said they would look forward to this but they didn't want to intrude on her and Jason's quality time together.

Jason sat looking very smug. "What more can a man hope for – a beautiful, intelligent, loving and fit lady who is also a marvellous cook?"

Chapter 7

Marigold chose her engagement ring with a design of three small diamonds; she bought Jason, as a surprise, a latest-technology mobile phone, which had all extras. This would help him in his work and at home.

He was overwhelmed.

He had bought her a pair of small, gold stud earrings with a diamond ring to match. He knew Marigold didn't like big jewellery.

She adored it and told him how much she adored him.

They celebrated their engagement at a local hotel. Some of the guests booked rooms for the night. Maisie had been fetched from Cornwall, and she stayed with Yvonne. Jason in his evening suit looked devastatingly handsome and virile. Marigold wore a 1950-style off-the-shoulder backless dress. Her creamy, smooth skin was perfect.

When Jason saw her he had to use all his self-control to resist embarrassing himself and her. It was the first time she had deliberately projected her sex appeal especially for Jason. He recognised that.

He said, "Wow! Now, honey, how am I going to survive this evening?"

She smiled. "You will, darling."

Both looked as though they were going to burst with happiness.

The meal and speeches were followed by a dance, which Jason and Marigold led.

After the party, Jason and his parents took Marigold home. Jason went up in the elevator with her, and they kissed, but they were discreet because the security camera was on them!

He saw Marigold into her room and asked, "Honey, how is your dress staying up?"

"That's my secret," she whispered in his ear.

He laughed. "Sleep well – I doubt if I will!"

On the way home, Susan told Jason, "What a wonderful evening! Marigold looked quite different – very attractive in a more mature way. We forget she is only twenty-three. She will make the most beautiful bride."

They were all silent. Jason was thinking of the promise Marigold had given him for the following morning at Hounscliffe. He tried to picture her in her wedding dress – her innocence.

Susan came in with, "She is preparing herself to be your wife."

"There must be a God in Heaven," Jason said thoughtfully.

His parents would have fallen out of their seats had it not been for the belts. It was the very first time Jason had mentioned anything to do with religion.

"My faith has grown stronger since I have known Marigold," Sir Philip said.

They went quiet again.

Reaching home, Jason bade them goodnight and thanked them for everything. "I am going for a swim," he said.

Philip and Susan sat in their bedroom with a small whisky each, discussing the evening and how Jason had changed. They thanked God for Marigold.

Next morning Jason, Marigold, Maisie and Nelson travelled on the train to Cornwall, where a hired car was waiting for them. They took Maisie home before going on to Hounscliffe. The workmen had left at lunchtime.

Jason made a coffee whilst Marigold lit the fires in their bedroom and the lounge. Marigold sat on Jason's lap whilst they drank their coffee.

Marigold said, "I long to be in your arms."

"I am hungry for you, sweetheart, but I'm not going to cause you any regrets; when you come to me in your white wedding dress I will be proud."

Marigold told him, "I will adore you for all of my life."

"I can't believe I am saying this, but come on, darling – ring Maisie. Ask if you can stay with her tonight. I will sleep here, and we will follow this pattern until we come together as a married couple."

"Let's have a walk in the garden. I'll just light the range ready to pop a casserole in." (Maisie was coming back with them for the meal.)

They went to see what progress had been made upstairs: the en-suite had been installed. It was magnificent; the room was decorated. The other bathrooms had been updated and all the tiles replaced; they were thrilled with the handiwork.

"Come on, darling – let's grab a sandwich and then take Maisie to thank them."

In the car, Jason told Maisie the truth: "We had planned, now we are engaged, to spend weekends here to have sex," he said.

"When we got here, Nanny, Jason refused me. He said he loved me too much to risk my having regrets. We are getting married in a few weeks so we will wait until then. This is why I need to sleep at your home tonight, and whenever we come down to check the workmen's progress."

"I am very proud of you both," Maisie told them. "Marigold, your parents would also be so proud."

They went to thank the workmen and Jason paid for the work done so far.

The owner told them, "The workmen are taking special pride in this work. We will be completing over the next two weeks."

Jason and Marigold thanked them again.

Next, they went to Geoff's and asked him to thank the men. They were pleased with the progress so far.

Geoff assured them they were pulling the stops out to get the outside work done whilst they were enjoying the good weather. "Do you want me to ask them to work tomorrow?"

Marigold said, "Yes please. As you say, get it done whilst the weather is so good."

Jason also paid him for the work his men had done. When they got back in the car, Jason said to Marigold and Maisie, "So far, so good. Are you all right, Maisie?" he asked. "If you are fed up, please tell us."

"Not at all! I am greatly enjoying myself. I enjoy every hour I spend with Marigold."

"I enjoy being with you, dearest Nanny."

They bought fresh vegetables to go with the casserole, and what they would need for breakfast the following morning. Maisie assured them she had everything in for the Sunday lunch she would be cooking for them before they caught the train home.

Marigold drove up to Hounscliffe early to cook Jason and herself breakfast. He told her the workmen had arrived at 7 a.m. He had made them a coffee.

Marigold laughed. "It's a good job they didn't catch us!"

Geoff tapped on the door, saying, "That smells good, Miss Carlisle."

"Thank you. Would you like a sandwich?"

"If you can spare it, please."

"Yes, I have bought plenty of bread. Would your friends like one?"

They all came to the door. "Yes please, Miss."

Jason asked, "Would you like a coffee?"

"Yes please, but may we have it not as strong?"

Jason laughed. "Sorry – I like it strong in the morning."

They took Nelson down to the beach and had a good walk. The weather was gorgeous.

"We had better check the washing machine, now Gordon has reminded me," said Jason.

They went into the utility room, where there was an old washing machine.

"This will perhaps do for the sports clothes and anoraks, but we need a new one and a dryer," Marigold reflected.

"Choose whatever you need from the London store, and whilst they are delivering they will be able to also bring the machines down. Then we can arrange for the local plumber to install them."

"Good thinking!" approved Marigold.

On their way back in the train they discussed what they still needed for Hounscliffe. Jason suggested they buy everything from the London store; they would deliver and assemble. Marigold welcomed this to give them more time.

Before having dinner at Jason's they had a swim.

Jason, with Marigold's permission, told his parents about the weekend. They were astounded! They said they wouldn't have had such self-control! They all laughed.

Next day, Marigold told her aunt, who said, "I have the greatest respect for both of you." She regretted Marigold's parents were not there to hear this, and she regretted her own life and her lack of self-control.

They both wept.

Chapter 8

Jason rang Marigold on the Wednesday. The estate agent had faxed him: 'A 16-bedroom Georgian manor house situated near Hampstead, North London, is coming on the market. It appears to fit all the boxes you require.'

"We need to talk about this, honey."

"Of course, darling. This sounds exciting. See you later. Love you."

"Love you, honey," he replied. Then he rang off.

Marigold was cooking for Jason.

When he arrived, after kissing her he told her how much Brierley Manor was being sold for.

"Wow!" Marigold exclaimed. "It must be a lovely house."

He showed her the brochure, and they sat down with a glass of wine.

Brierley Manor included sixty acres of land, with woodland at the back of the house, a swimming pool, tennis courts, a lake and beautiful lawns. Behind the house there were stables for eight horses.

"After buying Hounscliffe, honey, I haven't enough money for Brierley Manor; but if it is suitable for us, I will be able to get a mortgage. I'm on a good salary. Alternatively, I could sell Hounscliffe."

Marigold heard him out, then she took hold of his hand and said, "Darling, no. Thankfully from my grandparents and parents I received lots of money, which was invested for me. I also received a trust fund when I was twenty-one, plus my sister's and brothers' shares, which I also invested. I will get the latest figures tomorrow, but I will easily be able to put 75% towards Brierley Manor. It sounds perfect for you and me – and, prayerfully, our future children."

Jason was speechless. He had no idea Marigold had this kind of money.

"Also, darling, I will be selling this apartment. As you know, I paid a vast amount for it."

Jason pulled her on to his knee. "I can't believe it, darling honey," he said. "I had no idea you had this amount of money. Am I lucky – a rich future wife who is a gorgeous sexy lady *and* a wonderful cook! How good is that!"

Marigold smacked his hand.

"Is the meal ready, sweetheart?"

"Smells like it!" she laughed.

They kissed passionately. Jason was still dazed.

He rang the estate agent's and left a message asking them to arrange when he and Miss Carlisle could view Brierley Manor.

The agent arranged with the owners for them to visit on the following Saturday morning. They had first opportunity – it hadn't gone on the market yet. Jason was enabled not to go in to work.

When they arrived at Brierley Manor, the caretaker let them through the gates. When they saw the house they were thrilled. It was built of Cotswold stone, and there were three storeys. Everything was as in the brochure.

Lord and Lady Sutcliffe came to meet them and invited them in. Lady Sutcliffe had had a bad fall. Her horse had refused to jump a hedge and had thrown her. She had damaged her back and arthritis was setting in.

Lord Sutcliffe told them, "We are moving to Spain to be in a warmer climate."

Marigold and Jason expressed their sorrow and said they hoped Lady Sutcliffe would quickly recover.

The housekeeper brought coffee.

"I am a barrister; Miss Carlisle is a fashion designer," said Jason.

Lady Sutcliffe was delighted. "I know of your designing, Miss Carlisle. I congratulate you."

Jason then told them, "We are getting married early in December."

Lord and Lady Sutcliffe wished them all happiness, and Lady Sutcliffe then suggested they went to look round inside and out.

Inside the house was full of light. The large hall had a marble floor. Stairs led up from the half-landing to the left and right. There was a big country kitchen with an enormous Aga, a twelve-ring gas cooker and a big wooden kitchen table. Everywhere was spotless. Fourteen of the bedrooms had en-suite bathrooms, and there were wonderful views from the big windows. All the rooms were large. The more they saw, the more they liked.

When they had been shown round the property, Jason and Marigold said they were interested in buying, depending on the surveys. The estate agent had promised to get these to them on the following Monday.

Lady Sutcliffe invited them to stay for lunch if they could spare the time. They accepted with pleasure.

"It is chicken casserole today, if that is all right. Otherwise the chef will prepare something else."

"Thank you, that will be lovely."

Marigold told Jason, "I feel at home here already!"

Jason agreed: "I do also."

Before the meal Jason and Marigold were permitted to wander unaccompanied in the grounds.

He rang his mother: "Are you and Dad free tomorrow afternoon to view, if it is OK with Lord and Lady Sutcliffe?"

"Yes, of course we will be. Are you inviting Uncle Trevor and Aunt Anna also?"

"Naturally we are."

When they met up again for lunch, Jason asked Lord Sutcliffe, "May my parents, aunt and uncle come tomorrow afternoon?"

"Of course. We have heard of Sir Philip."

They enjoyed a relaxed lunch.

"I have bought my childhood holiday home in Polzeath, and we go down at weekends when our work permits," Jason said.

"Yes, we love it and my ex-nanny is living nearby," Marigold told them.

Jason explained, "Whilst Marigold was holidaying with her nanny, I stayed at the Rock Hotel. Then one Sunday afternoon, on a run into the countryside, we saw it was up for sale!"

"It is lovely. We are having alterations made, and we will honeymoon there. Then our relations are coming to spend Christmas with us. They will stay at the Rock Hotel because all our rooms will not be completed, but we will be together," Marigold excitedly said.

Jason proudly told them, "Marigold is a cordon-bleu cook; she learnt at finishing school."

"Yes, at Hounscliffe there is a big log- or coal-fired range; I am looking forward to cooking the turkey in it. I'm sorry – I must be boring you."

"Not at all, darling! You are very refreshing. Unfortunately we do not have children, but we have nephews and nieces. My sister would agree with me: if only they had your enthusiasm! All they think about is the next party and having silly fun. They have been spoilt. I can see your parents brought you up sensibly."

"Unfortunately," Jason explained, "Marigold's parents, paternal grandparents, elder sister and younger twin brothers were killed in their car by a drunken driver. Marigold would have been with them, but she had measles so she was at home with her nanny."

Lord and Lady Sutcliffe were so sorry.

"How tragic, darling! What happened then?" Lady Sutcliffe asked.

Marigold told her.

"Well, darling, your parents would be very proud of you. What I would like to say, darlings, is I have been feeling so sorry for myself after my accident that I have made poor Geoffrey's life a misery. Then when you tell me how brave you have been, growing up without your parents and family, I realise how terribly selfish I am. I am alive; I have staff to look after me; I have Geoffrey, who puts up with me."

Her husband broke in: "I married you, darling, for better or worse."

They all laughed.

Jason asked, "Please do not think me rude, but have you had specialist treatment on your back?"

"Yes, I had private care. It is a combination of arthritis and trapped nerves."

Jason went on: "I mentioned my father, Sir Philip – he is an eminent surgeon."

71

"Yes, we have heard of him."

"I wonder if possibly he and his team would be able to help."

"We would be grateful for any help. When he comes here tomorrow will it be good etiquette to ask him?"

"If he can help anyone, he will," promised Jason. "We must now let you rest, Lady Sutcliffe, and we thank you for your time and the lovely lunch."

"Yes – thank you very much," Marigold echoed.

"We want you to know we have enjoyed your company," Lord Sutcliffe told them.

"Pending the surveys, Marigold and I are very interested in buying Brierley Manor. I will be in trouble for this, but Marigold is paying 75%. As I have recently bought Hounscliffe I would have had to have a mortgage, which would not, with my salary, have been a problem, but I suggested to Marigold that I sell it. I felt guilty buying Hounscliffe, but it was a wonderful opportunity and it appeared to be no coincidence our coming across it as we did. I never dreamed a wonderful home like this would be offered to us."

Marigold told them, "It is naughty of Jason to have told you. I have been greatly blessed with money from my paternal and maternal grandparents as well as my parents, and everything being carefully invested. They would be so happy to know I will be living in a beautiful home with my beloved husband and – prayerfully – children."

They told her, with tears in their eyes, "Good! We will be happy for you to live here. Are you hoping to have many children?"

"Oh yes," Marigold replied, "lots – especially little boys with black curly hair and mischievous green eyes."

Jason said, "Also, we must have little girls like Marigold."

They all laughed.

Jason told them, "We will have an indoor swimming pool and a gym built. We both keep fit. We will also have an organic vegetable garden with a greenhouse."

Marigold laughed. "We will want to keep our children healthy."

Lord Sutcliffe informed them, "The farmer nearby is retiring soon, and he mentioned to me he will be selling off some fields."

Jason asked, "Where are they, sir?"

"As you come through our gates they are on the right-hand side. Take a look when you go out. Mr Greetham is probably at home now; I'm sure he would be happy to see you if you have time to call on him."

Jason looked at Marigold; she nodded.

"We are planning to dine with my parents and we were going to have a swim first, but sorting this opportunity out is top priority; we can swim any time."

Lord Sutcliffe gave them directions to the farm. He and Lady Sutcliffe came out with Jason and Marigold and waved them off.

"See you tomorrow, darlings," Lady Sutcliffe called.

She said to Geoffrey, "What a lovely couple! How well bred! They adore each other. I do hope the survey shows all is well with this house; I would love to see them living here."

"I am confident there is nothing wrong, darling, but Mr Norton is a barrister and they are both intelligent and realistic, so they need to make sure all is well. It is a vast amount of money they will be paying out. It's only what you and I would do."

"You are right, sweetheart."

When Jason and Marigold arrived at the farm, Mr and Mrs Greetham were outside. They introduced themselves and invited Jason and Marigold into the beautiful old farmhouse kitchen, where there was a big range and a log fire. They invited them to sit in front of the fire, and Mrs Greetham offered them a cup of tea.

Jason explained: "We are getting married early in December."

Mr and Mrs Greetham congratulated them.

"Pending the surveys being satisfactory, we intend to buy Brierley Manor."

"Brierley Manor?" Mr Greetham asked in amazement. "This is the first I have heard of it being sold."

"Yes," said Jason, "Lord and Lady Sutcliffe are moving to Spain in the hope that Lady Sutcliffe's back will be more comfortable in the warmer climate."

"Well, I never did!" the farmer said. "That was a terrible fall she had – such a beautiful lady!"

Jason explained: "As Miss Carlisle and I are getting married, we asked the estate agents to begin looking for a suitable home for us and, prayerfully, in time our family. They let us know Brierley was coming on the market, so that is how we came to be there viewing the property."

"Of course, sir – it's just that it's been a bit of a shock."
Marigold apologised.

"We mentioned we would be having an organic kitchen garden, and Miss Carlisle would like to keep chickens for eggs and for eating. That is when Lord Sutcliffe mentioned that you might be selling some fields adjoining their land."

"Aye, that's right, sir. I'm retiring. I have worked all my life, and now there is no money in farming. My sons all have a trade; they are doing well. They're not interested in farming as they can earn more money in their present jobs. We will continue to live on this farm, and I will grow vegetables and keep a few chickens for the eggs, but that's all."

"It is very sensible to have some time to yourselves after a lifetime of work."

"Yes, Miss, but the missus won't want me under her feet all day."

"No," she laughed, "he will only be bored and grumbling about everything."

They all laughed.

"So," Jason went on, "if, as I said, the surveys are OK, we would be interested in buying your fields."

Marigold came in with, "We would like to have a few sheep and cows for meat. Also, we need a field for Jason's horse. We have a holiday home in Cornwall, and we buy delicious organic meats, chickens, vegetables and eggs there. I would love to produce our own."

"Will you be cooking when you are married, Miss? Don't mind me asking," Mrs Greetham said.

"I will be. I love cooking – especially using the range in Cornwall. It's similar to yours. I'll cook some meals, but I will continue working. I am a fashion and wallpaper designer."

"That's it, Miss! I was wondering where I had seen you before. You have been on the television and in the papers and magazines."

"Yes," she laughed.

"You also make clothes for young people; our granddaughters have some of these."

Marigold explained: "I don't actually sew them; I design them, choose the materials and suggest the accessories."

Jason sat, pride in her shining out of him. He said, "When we are married, Miss Carlisle will cook when we go down to our holiday home. She cooks to cordon-bleu standard."

"Oh, Miss, that's lovely."

"I expect you cook as well as I do, Mrs Greetham."

Jason then said, "She makes wonderful healthy bread."

"Now I will continue with the bread. If I have a problem or am stressed, and work isn't going well, when I mix bread everything sorts itself out."

"Yes," Mrs Greetham agreed, "I know exactly what you mean. Would you both like a fresh cuppa?"

"Yes please."

Mr Greetham said, "I have been thinking, sir, Miss, if you agree, when you have thought, I could see to the cows, sheep and chickens for you for a small wage. I will be getting a pension so I can't earn too much, but that would get me out of the house and give me an interest. The caretaker and housekeeper at Brierley are friends of mine so they would vouch for my honesty. You could buy my cows and sheep as well if you want. They are all healthy. In fact, the cows will be delivering soon."

Jason said, "That sounds all right – doesn't it, honey?"

"It sounds brilliant. You will appreciate we are both busy. Mr Norton is a barrister."

"Right, Mr Greetham," Jason said, "we will be in touch early next week after we have received, as mentioned before, a satisfactory survey. May I have your telephone number?"

"Of course, sir, but you need have no fears about Brierley – it's only thirty years old. Lord and Lady Sutcliffe have been the only owners, and they have had it looked after. It was built to the highest quality. It must be worth a penny or two."

"Yes," laughed Jason, "it is. We had better not waste any more of your time. Thank you for the lovely tea and your promise of helping us."

"Would you like a couple of fresh rabbits, Miss, and some vegetables and eggs?"

"Oh, yes please," Marigold asked eagerly. "I cook quite a lot in my apartment for the freezers and Mr Norton and his family."

"Oh, you don't live together, then?" Mr Greetham queried.

Mrs Greetham admonished him: "You don't ask questions like that of the gentry, Ned."

He apologised. "No offence meant, sir, Miss. I was just surprised. It's unusual not to these days."

Jason said, "We will live together when we are married, of course."

"Oh, yes, sir, of course."

Jason and Marigold laughed.

Mr Greetham fetched them the rabbits, vegetables and eggs.

Marigold paid him. "I confess I haven't cooked rabbit before; I will look in my recipe books," she said.

"No problem, Miss," Mrs Greetham advised. "Just put them in a casserole dish with plenty of pearl barley, vegetables and lentils, then cook slowly. When cooked, pop little dumplings on the top and continue cooking until they are raised and light."

Ned promised, "I could supply you with vegetables and eggs, Miss, until you get set up. I could leave them with the caretaker. In the wood at night there are poachers, but they are harmless. Lord Sutcliffe knows about them. They are village men who cannot get work or need a bit extra. They keep the rabbits down but move their traps before morning. This is a safe area.

Young miss could walk through that wood in the middle of the night by herself and not come to any harm. The poachers would be out of sight, keeping a protective watch over her."

Marigold and Jason laughed.

"We have enjoyed being with you. We will be in touch very shortly," Jason said.

The Greethams came out with them and waved goodbye.

"That's a turn-up for the books, Brierley being sold," said Mr Greetham when they had gone. "I'll just nip down to the pub while you cook tea, Ruth."

"I thought you wouldn't be able to wait to tell your pals."

"I need to make enquiries about how much to charge for the fields, Ruth."

That couple – you can tell they are posh, but they will stand no nonsense. It will be grand to have them in our community. Fancy them not living together!"

"We didn't before we married," Ruth reminded him.

"Aye, that's right, we didn't," Ned replied, and as he left he said, "They must have a bob or two."

He told his pals in the pub about the visit. "Mr Norton is a barrister and Miss Carlisle a fashion designer. They want to buy my fields and animals. They believe in having everything organic."

They laughed at that.

"I suppose when they have been cooped up all day they need to get into the fresh air," someone suggested.

They all agreed.

Jason and Marigold returned to Brierley Manor the next afternoon with their family. After Lord and Lady Sutcliffe greeted them, they went viewing. They loved everywhere. They went in for afternoon tea.

"Jason has put me in the picture, Lady Sutcliffe, about the injuries to your back. What exactly did your surgeon tell you?" Philip asked.

Geoffrey explained in detail; Philip listened intently.

"Yes, I am afraid there is no other way, other than to adhere to what Sir Thomas has said. I'm deeply sorry about this, but I would willingly meet with Sir Thomas if he agreed to discuss this case with me."

Geoffrey said, "We would be grateful for any help."

"At St Justin's", Philip said thoughtfully, "we do have the latest technology. Please ask Sir Thomas, if he agrees to meet me, to contact me there."

Geoffrey and Amelia, as they had asked them to call them, thanked him.

Philip then said, "We are all very impressed with your home. It is beautiful."

Susan endorsed that.

"We are now awaiting the surveys, but we do not anticipate any problems."

"We appreciate Marigold and Jason inviting us – and we are grateful for your hospitality – but it is their decision," Susan stated.

"I can speak for Marigold: we love it here," said Jason. "We feel at home already. It will make a lovely home for us."

The survey showed no problems. Uncle Trevor asked an estate-agent friend, after showing him the brochure, "Is it worth this price?"

"It is, most definitely; in fact, they could easily have asked and got more."

Marigold and Jason bought it.

Geoffrey invited, "When we have sorted out the furniture for Spain, if there is anything you would like, we will be happy to let you buy."

They thanked him and Amelia.

"Are you taking the piano, Lady Sutcliffe?" Marigold asked.

"No darling, I am unable to play. Would you like it?"

Marigold looked at Jason. He smiled. "Yes please! May I try it?"

It was very satisfactory.

Amelia asked Marigold to play for them.

"What would you like?"

Amelia asked for her favourite classic piece. Marigold knew it.

Jason sat listening and marvelling at her. He was overflowing with pride and love for her. They thanked her.

Geoffrey said positively, "We will buy another in Spain when you are ready, darling."

To celebrate the sale, Marigold invited all of them to dinner in her apartment. She asked if they liked fresh rabbit.

Only Amelia and Geoffrey could remember ever having had it (made from rabbits caught on their land).

Marigold told them Mrs Greetham had given her some.

Philip's chauffeur fetched Geoffrey and Amelia. Susan made Amelia very comfortable with cushions in her chair for the meal.

It was a wonderful atmosphere, and the four-course meal was, as always, cooked to perfection by Marigold. They loved the rabbit casserole with the healthy ingredients she had put in and tiny fluffy dumplings.

Jason asked, "May I have some bread to soak up the gravy?" so they all had some!

Philip laughingly said, "Some of our friends wouldn't believe us if we told them!"

After the meal Marigold and Jason took Amelia and Geoffrey into the lounge. Marigold played for them, as they had requested. The others cleared the table, washed up and put everything clean back on the table. Jason set the coffee machine going.

After coffee, they all had a whisky. Then the chauffeur arrived. They all kissed and thanked Marigold.

Amelia tearfully asked, "Please keep in touch. We are so pleased to know all of you."

They promised they would.

Philip and Sir Thomas discussed Lady Sutcliffe's back. Philip studied the X-rays carefully. There was extensive damage where she had fallen at an awkward angle.

Philip asked, "Is it worth opening her up again and perhaps supporting the bones a little more?"

"I would be glad of any advice, Sir Philip."

Philip said, "I would like a colleague of mine to see these X-rays."

"Please do whatever you can. She is a lovely lady, and I would do anything to ease her pains and also help Lord Sutcliffe. This accident has devastated both their lives."

Philip's colleague examined the X-rays at length and admitted that with all the damage there wasn't much he could suggest, but he agreed they could try supporting the spine with a stainless-steel part!

They met with Geoffrey and Amelia.

Sir Thomas urged, "Please don't raise your hopes too much. The damage is extensive, but we hope we will ease the pressure and pain by inserting a piece of stainless steel."

Geoffrey begged, "Please do anything to help."

Amelia echoed that.

"There will be no danger and, one way or another, with medication and the warmth of the Spanish climate, prayerfully we will make your lives less stressful."

They performed the operation, and it *did* ease the pains a little, but, regretfully, it wasn't a cure. Philip reassured them that he and his colleagues would continue enquiring for any new technology and they would all pray.

Amelia asked, "Please come to visit us soon."

Philip promised, "We certainly will make the time."

Chapter 9

Marigold suggested to Jason, "After we are married I could do some of the cooking."

"Darling, being married to me, continuing work, running a household – you will have more than enough on for now. Let's get married and settled in. When you start with the babies you will be able to cook with the kitchen help."

"Thank you, darling. You are right as always."

"Good!" laughed Jason. "I am glad you think that."

She kissed him.

"When we go to Hounscliffe for weekends, if you want to cook then, that will be enough for you, honey."

The housekeeper, chef, his assistant, the caretaker and other staff had asked to stay on. They were all absolutely trustworthy.

Yvonne gave Marigold a generous money gift and told her, "Everything eventually will be yours, Marigold."

She thanked her aunt and pleaded, "Not for years and years, please, darling Tante."

With the money they installed an indoor swimming pool with a separate shallow pool for the future children to splash about safely in. Also shower changing rooms and a separate gym were built at the back of Brierley Manor.

Whilst Philip was playing golf with Susan, Trevor and Anna, he said, "I have been thinking about Clarissa, and really I now feel guilty about our twins. I haven't spent any time with them these last few years. They have spent their holidays from boarding school with their friends, and now they are at university we don't even see them at Christmas; they stay with their friends."

Susan agreed: "That's true, Philip. What can we do?"

Trevor came in with, "What about renting Hounscliffe from Jason and Marigold some weekends and holidays? Lord and Lady Sutton, the parents of their friends Dominic and Stephen have their holiday home nearby, so they could meet up. There are so many sports in Cornwall as well as great places for walking."

"You are right," Philip agreed. "Good one, Trev! We must ask Jason and Marigold first."

Jason and Marigold were delighted at this news. They were pleased that Hounscliffe would give them all pleasure.

Philip told them, "We will pay – you have a lot on."

"You will most certainly not," Marigold firmly said. "You are our family."

Jason joked smugly, "Yes, we have Marigold's money. I'm sorry, Uncle Trevor, she hasn't been able to invest as yet." "She has done better in buildings than in stocks and shares."

"We want to settle in our new home and not go to Hounscliffe every weekend just yet. Please feel free to use it whenever you are able. Also I will not want Marigold to travel all that way when she is pregnant."

Susan was thrilled. "That is very thoughtful of you, Jason," she said. "Marigold is so precious to all of us, and you will have beautiful children."

Philip rang the twins and asked them, "Would you like to go to Hounscliffe with us for the weekend? Dominic and Stephen's parents have bought a holiday home nearby."

They were speechless but managed, "Thanks, Dad! Brill! We're sorry we haven't rung you and Mum lately and spent time with you. We would love to go to Hounscliffe."

Philip told them, "Your mother and I feel we have neglected you both these last few years."

"That's OK; we've been busy with our studies and our friends. We'll make our own way there on the train."

Susan smiled. "We'll take our chef with us if you don't mind. He will not want to use your range, Marigold, but thank goodness there is the gas oven!"

As a wedding present, Philip and Susan suggested they buy Jason and Marigold settees and armchairs for the Brierley lounge. "Please look around and choose what you will like, and then we will have them made," said Philip.

"Thank you. We will when we have chosen the patterned wallpaper for around the fireplace." (They had a large open fire.)

Marigold designed the wallpaper and had curtains made incorporating the same pattern. At Philip and Susan's request, she and Jason chose two four-seater settees (one hard, one soft), two two-seater settees (again one hard, one soft), six armchairs and two matching footstools. Work on these would start immediately, they were promised. They would be able to add to this order later if needed.

Anna and Trevor bought them a dining table to seat forty plus chairs. In accordance with Jason and Marigold's wishes, they matched the cupboard Marigold had bought for her apartment to display her parent's china and the rare crystal glasses.

Yvonne bought them a king-sized bed and a daybed, which they chose, complete with the best quality bedding.

Yvonne asked Marigold to meet with her. "I ask you, darling, if you would, to accept a partnership with me. You have brought so much business into the shop with your designs and reputation. The business will be all yours eventually, of course, darling. Please talk it over with Jason. When you are married you could work from home and come here part-time, thereby preparing for when you have your babies. And, darling, the business has expanded so much; I suggest we get an accountant in. I appreciate you will be running your home and doing the accounts. Your maths skills will not be wasted."

Marigold was amazed. "Thank you, Tante," she said. "I will have, as you say, enough on without the shop accounts. I was going to ask you about this. My maths degree will not be wasted, as you sensibly point out, Tante. I will be running Brierley and then, prayerfully, I will be able to help our children with their schoolwork. I do also have to work out measurements for outfits, materials, trimmings, etc."

"Of course, darling Marigold, this all takes brains."

"I also would appreciate the accountant helping me with my accounts and the income tax from my designing jobs," Marigold added. "I do love you, and I am so grateful to you, Tante. I want you to be happy and enjoy your life."

"I enjoy my life now with you, dearest. I never dreamed such joy and peace existed until you came from Paris. Think carefully and let me know when you have decided, darling."

Whilst out walking, Marigold told Jason of her meeting with Yvonne.

He asked, "Will it mean taking on more responsibility than you have now?"

"I wouldn't think so. In fact, it will be easier for me without the accounts and with the PA now taking over the administration. I have suggested the accountant could also take care of my separate business accounts and income tax. I will be able to concentrate on the designing. I would love to continue this after we marry, also the wallpapers. As I mentioned to Tante, I will be using my maths degree with the running of Brierley accounts – and you will not know this probably, Jason: it takes maths skills to sort out measurements for materials and trimmings for my outfits and hats."

Jason admitted, "No, I had never thought of that side of it, honey. Yvonne must have thought this out carefully in the light of our coming marriage. She is right: there are plenty of rooms with good light at Brierley for you and your colleagues to work in. I would like to think of you being at home but doing what makes you happy, sweetheart. Your languages skills will also continue to be put to good use, dealing with the people you meet in your work and shows. I am so proud of you, but I am humbled by the way you consider me before taking any decision. You are a gorgeous lady and so is Yvonne."

"Will you tell Tante that you think she is a gorgeous lady, darling? It will boost her confidence."

"I will, honey."

They held each other and kissed. People passing were good-humouredly whistling.

They laughed.

"May we ask Uncle Trevor to recommend an accountant? And I will continue to invest my salaries."

"Good idea, honey! Let's meet up with Yvonne to discuss this first.

Yvonne came to Marigold's apartment for dinner, and afterwards she, Marigold and Jason had a round-table conference. They celebrated with champagne.

Marigold invited Jason's parents, Anna, Trevor, Yvonne and Maisie, whom Jason had the chauffeur fetch up on that Thursday to stay with Tante, to Friday evening dinner in her apartment. At Marigold's request the chauffeur brought up chickens, meats, eggs and vegetables from the organic farm.

After a delicious meal (as they expected from Marigold), Jason brought out bottles of champagne and Yvonne told them the good news that she and Marigold were now going to be partners. They were all delighted.

Marigold explained: "We are now getting an accountant in, Uncle Trev. I hope you will recommend one also to sort my wallpaper business and the chain-store designs accounts. Also, I need someone to help me with the dreaded income tax!"

Trevor reassured her and Yvonne: "I will be delighted to help you both in any way I can."

"Marigold will still be using her maths degree," said Jason. "I had no idea until she explained to me that it takes maths skills to work out measurements for materials for the outfits and hats."

They all agreed they hadn't thought of that aspect of designing.

Jason also added, "And when, prayerfully, our children are doing their homework, they will be so blessed to have an intelligent mother to help them!"

Marigold then went on: "I will continue investing part of my salaries, Uncle Trev."

Yvonne suggested, "I am speaking without consulting Marigold," – they all clapped – "but we must discuss asking Trevor about investing our profits when he has time. If Trevor agrees, we will have him attend to everything. This is a new beginning, and my investors will appreciate this without being upset. Everything one day will be Marigold's."

Jason told them, "Marigold and I have discussed that she will work 70% of her time at Brierley. There are plenty of rooms with good light that can be made into workrooms and offices for her colleagues. I would like to think of Marigold being at home with the household. When we start having babies this will be much easier for her. She will be able to design at her own pace."

Yvonne said, "This is another wonderful blessing because the workshops are really too small for all the business we now do, thanks to Marigold."

"I have just had a thought: do we have to pay anything to use Brierley as a workplace?" Marigold mused.

Trevor said, "That is a good query. I will certainly look into it, but I don't think there will be a problem. It's a private paid-up residence."

"I will enquire among my colleagues," Jason promised. "We had better not break the law!"

They laughed at this. They congratulated Yvonne. "Well done, Yvonne!" Then they all clapped her.

Jason brought out the most beautiful bouquet of flowers and gave this to her with a kiss on her cheek. He told her, "You are a gorgeous lady, Yvonne."

They clapped again!

Jason set the coffee machine going. They all carried everything through to the kitchen and washed, dried and put everything away. Maisie was astounded.

Susan said, "We are getting used to this, Maisie."

They all went into the lounge and had coffee. Marigold sat on Jason's knee.

When the contracts had been signed, Yvonne and Marigold put the announcement into the newspapers and magazines, mentioning that after Marigold was married she would work from Brierley Manor. It was also broadcast on the television stations.

Congratulations, best wishes and gifts poured in.

Chapter 10

It was time to complete the wedding arrangements. Susan and Anna sent out the invitations to just close friends and others who expected to be invited. The arrangements went smoothly. The wedding presents were displayed at Susan and Philip's home. Jason arranged to live with Marigold in her apartment after the wedding until they moved to Brierley Manor.

When he had the time in his lunch hour, Jason went round the jewellers' shops looking for an idea of what he could buy Marigold for a wedding present. He had bought jewellery for his former girlfriends, but Marigold only liked dainty jewellery. He thought and then had a gold chain made with a pendant of three small diamonds to match her engagement ring. He was happy with this, and he told Yvonne what he had planned. Then he asked her to help him with ideas for another present.

She suggested her dressmakers make Marigold a nightdress and negligee in Italian silk.

"But this, darling, will be for my pleasure," Jason said with a laugh.

"Well, there we are – a present to please both of you!" She also laughed. She loved Jason. A pang went through her. If only, when she was younger, she had met someone like him!

"Right," Jason said, "let's go for it. Will three be enough?"

"Yes." Yvonne laughed again, thinking they would not get much wear. "Leave it with me."

For early December it was a glorious morning, fine with the sun breaking through the clouds. The old church was full of flowers and perfume. Marigold of course had designed her dress and veil, and she wore her mother's inherited diamond tiara. She had also designed all the men's cravats.

Robert, Jason's soldier brother, had leave previously due to him to be Jason's best man. Maisie had been fetched up to stay with Yvonne.

Yvonne proudly led Marigold up to Jason at the altar. His eyes filled with tears of thankfulness when he saw Marigold in all her beauty coming towards him. He was so thankful that he had practised self-control and not given in to his lust. Marigold looked pure and innocent, ready to make her vows before God. Jason looked magnificent. He took her breath away.

Marigold had been weeping that morning. She was upset that her grandparents, parents, sister and brothers would not be there with her.

Television companies had asked if they might film. Jason and Marigold gave them permission, but not in church – outside if they so wished. They did.

Alan, one of Jason's friends, with their permission had set up a camera to discreetly record the wedding. He filmed everyone arriving at the church, but during the service he only filmed the backs of Jason and Marigold as they took their vows.

More photographers and cameramen were outside. They had filmed the family and the famous guests, Jason, and then Marigold arriving. Jason and Marigold good-naturedly posed for the photographers.

They had a wonderful reception at the same local hotel as they had used for their engagement; the weather was still good enough to take photographs outside.

After the reception, Marigold and Jason changed, and Joseph took them, Maisie and Nelson down to Cornwall. Joseph stayed overnight at the Rock Hotel.

The caretaker and his wife had lit fires in the lounge and bedroom, and the range. They greeted Jason and Marigold at the gates and wished them all happiness.

Inside, Marigold took hold of Jason's hand and led him upstairs; they undressed urgently. He carried her to their bed.

A few days later whilst walking on the beach with Nelson, Marigold asked, "Do you think our family would like to spend Christmas with us at Hounscliffe?"

"The rooms won't be ready, honey."

"No, darling, but I thought they could stay at the Rock Hotel and have Christmas meals with us."

"That sounds wonderful."

Marigold suggested, "You ask them, darling. I think if the invitation comes from you, they may find it easier to say no if they don't want to come."

"That's good thinking."

When they returned to the house he rang his mother.

She welcomed the invitation. "It will be wonderful all being together at Christmas," she said. "I do hope Robert will get home from Afghanistan. If not, we will send him a parcel – that's all we can do at the moment. The twins will love being there, walking and climbing; and if the weather is good, they will be able to do some surfing. Isn't Marigold lovely? It will be so wonderful having Christmas there in the country."

Susan asked to speak to Marigold, and she thanked her.

Marigold asked, "May I invite Tante?"

"Of course, darling. You don't have to ask me; it's your home."

Susan then asked, "Do you want our chef to come? I'm sure he will give up his holiday."

"Thank you, no. I will delight in doing the cooking. Maisie will help me. I can prepare and freeze certain items."

Susan promised, "We will do the washing-up."

"We must get the other rooms completed as soon as possible, so you can all come for holidays on your own or with the twins. I would prefer for our room not to be used."

"Marigold darling, we do love you, and we love your straight way of speaking. We are never afraid to say anything to you, because you would tell us if we are not right."

Marigold laughed. "I am so blessed to have you all as part of my family; there are plenty of other rooms."

Philip rang the Rock Hotel.

"We were going to close for Christmas because for the last

few years we have had only three couples. Now you, Sir Philip, and your family are coming we will remain open. We are overjoyed at this news."

"We will be having Christmas Eve dinner and Christmas Day meals at Hounscliffe. Other meals – we will let you know."

"Thank you, sir; we will be honoured to have you."

Jason and Marigold flew down four days previously to prepare; the hire car was waiting for them at the airport. Marigold had taken plenty of bread and other foodstuffs.

Maisie had told them of an organic farmer who would supply turkeys, potatoes and fresh vegetables. She rang and told him that Mr and Mrs Norton would be coming, and she gave him an idea of what they would need.

They went the next day with Maisie and ordered two very large turkeys, chickens, a piece of beef, ham and sausages.

Marigold said, "I can cook the turkeys in the big ovens at the same time, so we will have plenty. Any leftovers I can make into dishes and sandwiches."

The farmer promised to deliver the meat and vegetables.

Next they bought a tree; they had brought decorations from London, and later she and Jason gathered holly from their wood.

Maisie was overjoyed to be included in the family Christmas.

Jason admitted, "I have never made much of Christmas, so this one is especially precious to me."

It was lovely at Hounscliffe – the log fires, the comfortable new settees and chairs, and everything.

The family joined Jason and Marigold at 4 o'clock; they ate at 5 and then opened their presents and had a sing-song with Marigold playing the piano. They had all agreed on Marigold cooking Italian.

Stephen asked, "Are you coming to Christmas Midnight Communion with us?"

"Well, no, thank you. We don't want to leave Nelson by himself. There may be noisy fireworks."

Robert laughed. "I have heard some good excuses, but this is the best yet – you are on your honeymoon, after all!"

Marigold blushed; Jason put his arm round her.

"We are going with Maisie to the service tomorrow morning," he said.

They all kissed Marigold goodnight.

When they had left, Jason, Marigold and Nelson went for a walk in the grounds. The lights of the village were shining. They could hear carol-singers, and church bells ringing.

Jason breathed to Marigold, "Isn't it beautiful? I have never known a Christmas like this."

They stood in awe, looking up at the stars.

"I wonder what next Christmas will be like," mused Marigold.

"Well," teased Jason, "we could have a squawking baby, or you could have a delicious hump in front of you."

"Our babies will not squawk!" she protested.

"No, darling, they will not. They will be as beautiful as you are."

"You are beautiful, my precious darling husband. Shall we go in to do some more practising?"

"I thought you would never ask!"

They put plenty of coal on the fires and in the range to heat the ovens for the turkeys. Marigold had prepared them; Jason had put them on the cold slab in the cool larder.

Nelson curled up in his basket in front of the fireguard. He was very content.

On Christmas morning Jason gave Marigold an extra present: it was a beautiful eternity ring.

She loved it, but said, "Darling, I haven't bought you an extra present."

Jason just said, "Come here."

A taxi brought Maisie at 2 o'clock to help with last-minute jobs. The family came at 4.30 to the wonderful aroma of Christmas cooking.

Philip told them, "You can smell it half a mile away!"

Marigold had planned the meal for 5 o'clock to allow the twins to have a sports day with their friends, Dominic and Stephen, the teenage sons of Susan and Philip's friends Lord and Lady Sutton, who had recently bought a holiday home nearby.

They sat in the lounge in front of the giant log fire with a drink before the meal.

The twins and Robert washed up as Marigold filled the tureens. They said the obvious: "We are starving!"

Jason assured them, "There is plenty to go at."

The dining table looked spectacular. Jason carried one of the turkeys in; Trevor carved. He was an expert. Everyone helped carry in. Philip poured the wine.

The meal went smoothly. The turkey was succulent; they all said they had never tasted turkey as good.

Marigold laughed, "It's because it's organic and cooked in the range."

They made a start on the second one! Marigold brought in an extra tin of roast potatoes she had cooked "just in case". They were all so happy. They pulled crackers, put the paper hats on and read the silly jokes.

Then Jason brought in the pudding. He had covered it with brandy and so set it alight for the table. This frightened Nelson, who cowered under the table, trembling.

Jason told them, and asked, "May he come in, please?"

They all answered, "Of course. Poor Nelson!"

They made a fuss of him, and Jason gave him some of the turkey. By the time the meal was over, they were all so full that they didn't want to move.

The twins and Robert insisted they do the washing-up as they had promised Marigold. They put everything on the kitchen table for her to inspect.

Jason had bought an identical coffee machine to Marigold's, and he set it going. They all retired to the lounge, and later they had a walk round the garden to enjoy the beautiful early evening weather. Afterwards they all went back to watch the recorded Queen's Christmas message, and then listened to the Christmas carols from King's College.

Enjoying a brandy, Philip toasted Marigold and thanked her for the wonderful meal.

She protested: "You have all helped."

She accompanied Jason. He had a beautiful voice, and then

they all sang the popular Christmas carols.

After this they played a video brain game similar to Mastermind, and Nathan remarked, "You are very clever, Marigold." Then he asked her a difficult maths question.

She explained the answer.

"Wow!" he said. "That is a great help to me. If I'm in difficulty, may I fax you?"

Marigold answered, "Of course. I will not give you the answer, but I will do as I just have – helping you to work it out. That way you will remember."

"Thanks, sis," he said cheekily.

Marigold told them, "You have no idea how precious you are to me. My twin brothers, who would have been your age, were killed in a car accident."

"Yes, Jason has told us. We are so sorry." They came over and cuddled her.

Robert said, "We are very glad to have you in our family, Marigold – and not just because you are a good cook, although that is 80%."

They all laughed.

He said, "Trust our Jason to have pinched a wonderful lady like you, Marigold! Have you any friends like you?"

Marigold said, "There is Clarissa."

Jason groaned. "Not Clarissa!"

"She has changed. She is learning to cook! If you like, Robert, I will keep you posted."

"OK. Thank you."

They all laughed.

The weather was wonderful again on Boxing Day. It was springlike. After their walk they returned to Hounscliffe and made turkey, ham and pickle sandwiches with Marigold's home-made bread. As arranged, a taxi brought Maisie.

They had all been invited to dinner at Lord and Lady Sutton's. Their sons (Dominic and Stephen), the twins and Robert had been surfing all morning. Jason and Marigold had excused themselves from the meal to stay with Nelson!

When the others had gone, Jason and Marigold took Nelson out into the garden, enjoying another beautiful early part of the night.

Jason teased Marigold: "Do you realise we will not have to get up in the morning? No one is coming."

Marigold answered, "What if the painters come? They are eager to get on since the outside has been held up by the rain."

Jason groaned. "We had better keep our curtains closed."

The painters didn't come until the next day.

The family went back to London. Sir Philip had to return to the hospital, where he had several operations lined up. Jason and Marigold stayed on for another three days, putting the decorations and tree away, tidying up and walking on the beach with Nelson. Marigold supplied the painters with tea, coffee and sandwiches. Then they went to stay with Jason's parents for the New Year. Yvonne, of course had been invited. Maisie, as usual, was spending New Year with her neighbours.

Marigold received a card and letter from Clarissa:

> My three friends and I thank you for guiding us to the finishing school. We are enjoying it immensely and not getting into too much trouble! We are working hard.
>
> I have met a young politician with a good future in front of him. Mummy and Daddy have met him and his family and they approve.
>
> Mummy is getting quite big now with my little brother; they are so happy they are like teenagers.
>
> Best wishes to you all,
>   from Clarissa

Marigold cried when she had read it. She replied:

> Thank you, Clarissa, for your beautiful card and letter. Jason and I will be very pleased to see you as soon as convenient.
>
> Congratulations on meeting your boyfriend.
>
> I hope your mother remains well and has a safe delivery.
>
> All best wishes,
>   Marigold

A television producer asked Jason and Marigold if they would please give them an interview in their 9-p.m. chat show.

They thought about it and both agreed. "Why not?"

For the questions and suggestions they worked with the producer and presenter.

During this interview Jason teased Marigold, making her blush. Everyone could see he adored her. He looked gorgeous in his hand-made suit; his shirt was open at the neck. He had a most beautiful voice. Marigold wore a dress which she had designed herself. They had dressed up out of respect for the presenter and the programme.

Jason constantly praised her. He answered the presenter's question, "How did you meet, sir?" by saying, "I went to a charity dinner my mother and aunt were hosting. It was in June and the weather was hot. It had been stuffy in the courts and I really wanted to be in the fresh air, walking on the heath with my dog. I could have given them a donation, but out of respect for my mum and aunt's hard work I went. There I met Marigold." He sat back. They had been holding hands ever since the beginning of the interview, but he now put his arm round her waist. "I had never thought much about religion and that kind of thing, but meeting Marigold made me think that there must be a God guiding us."

They were all quiet for a few seconds.

"We are true soulmates," Jason added.

The presenter and crew noted how they listened to each other without interrupting.

They discussed Marigold's maths and finance degrees not being wasted with her working out measurements and costings for her materials and accessories; that she spoke in six languages, which was a great asset in the international fashion world; and about her being a cordon-bleu cook and making healthy bread.

The presenter went on to mention Brierley Manor, and asked if she and Jason had bought it between them.

"My grandparents and parents left me a good legacy," Marigold said.

They briefly talked about Hounscliffe, their holiday home.

"It's beautiful for us and our family," Marigold told him. "We have all been to spend Christmas there. It has been marvellous."

Jason agreed, smiling.

The presenter then asked, "Do you want children?"

Marigold answered, "Yes, we do – lots."

He laughed. "How many?"

"Lots!" She smiled at him.

Jason sat there, looking pleased and nodding.

"You support charities?"

"Yes, full stop," Jason said.

"Quite, sir! I apologise."

The presenter thanked them and hoped they would give another interview someday. They promised they would.

When they had finished, Jason disconnected Marigold's microphone and pulled her onto his lap. Unknown to them, the cameras recorded this. The ladies of the crew, even the ones happily married or with a partner, felt a pang of jealousy. Jason was so full of sex appeal. He was exciting. The men were thinking how beautiful Marigold was, with her shiny hair, beautiful skin, large brown eyes full of gold flecks, and her slim but curvy figure.

The presenter showed them the film clip and asked, "May we show this?"

"Of course! I have the world in my arms."

A picture was shown in the newspapers and all the magazines with the caption, 'Millionaire Jason has the world in his arms.'

Chapter 11

They moved into Brierley Manor at the beginning of January, and loved it. The sale of the fields went through, also the cows and sheep. These were brought into the fields. Jason didn't bring his horses up yet. One field was retained and made into a kitchen garden with a very long greenhouse incorporating all the latest technology of heating and watering. They advertised for an organic gardener and a young man to help.

Several people applied, and, after police and health checks, with Ned's approval they chose a local man in his early thirties and a young man, also from the village, who was learning the trade part-time at the local college.

The gardeners planted fruit trees and bushes and laid out plots, and the builders completed the paths and installed a very strong wire fence with concrete posts. Marigold had a plot laid out for the growing of flowers, and they decided to install a new chicken run.

Jason and Marigold both agreed they were getting off to a good start. Jason's family thought it was marvellous that they had this interest.

Jason teased Marigold: "We had better have plenty of organic food to make healthy babies."

She came back with, "There is nothing wrong with you in that department!"

They laughed, and he pulled her on to his knee.

"It's wonderful being married, isn't it?"

Marigold agreed. "I never ever dreamed such happiness was possible."

Ned oversaw the building of the chicken house and run and

the fencing-off to keep the foxes out. The twins, Nathan and Peter, had bought two cockerels, Bill and Ben.

Ned's friends in the pub kept asking if they could help. He told them he was the couple's right-hand man. Jason and Marigold were very fond of him and he made them laugh. The men from the village walked up the lane at the side of the fields watching all the progress being made. When Jason and Marigold met them they always had a conversation with them.

Ned suggested, "Why don't you have a few pigs?"

"Aren't they dirty?"

"Well – could be," Ned answered, "they do have to root in dirt but if they are cleaned out regularly, it needn't be a big problem."

"Fresh, succulent pork chops and our own home-made sausages!" Marigold said dreamily.

"Who would look after them, Ned?"

"I couldn't take that job on, but I daresay the local pig farmer would pop up daily and clean them out. They are no trouble to feed – just leave plenty of food and water. Shall I ask him?"

Marigold and Jason laughed. "What next, Ned?"

He took his cap off and scratched his head. "Well, you never know, Mrs Norton, but fresh is best."

They all laughed.

He arranged it for them.

The pig farmer met them in the field.

"Best be away at the top of the field," he advised. "Do you want me to have the pens made?"

"Yes please."

"How many pigs are you thinking of having?"

"How many do you suggest?"

"Six – then you will get plenty of piglets from them."

He arranged everything and brought two adult pigs and six piglets.

"They'll soon grow, sir, ma'am," he promised.

Next Ned suggested they rear their own turkeys. He arranged all this and he looked after them.

"You and Ruth will have plenty of our meat, Ned," Marigold promised.

He rubbed his hands together at this.

Jason and Marigold were requested to play an active part in the community. They asked to be excused for now; they were too busy with their careers and setting up home. Everyone understood. They were thrilled to have them at Brierley.

Marigold's designing continued to flourish. The teenagers loved her designs for casual outfits.

She and Jason cycled, walked or ran up the horseshoe concrete road around Brierley. It was well lit with electric lamps.

Marigold and her work colleagues cycled during their lunchtimes. For lunch she had fresh fruit and yoghurt.

After dinner she and Jason swam then soaked in their big bath, communicating.

In March she began with morning sickness. The scan showed twins. They didn't ask the sexes. Maisie came up to stay with her during the latter part of her pregnancy. She was healthy all the way through and had a quite easy delivery. She had kept fit by keeping up with gentle exercise such as walking. Marigold gave birth at home with private care. She was delivered of a boy (he had fair hair, with the look of her father, Colin) and a girl with black curls and green eyes! Both weighed in at just over 4 kilos. They were gorgeous; Marigold and Jason couldn't stop crying with joy.

Marigold then wept because her parents and family were not there to share their joy. Jason gently cuddled her.

They had hired maternity nurses to cover day and night.

The first time Jason saw her feeding the babies he looked at her with his 'special' look. She blushed. She had plenty of milk, and the babies suckled until her breasts were empty.

Jason laughed. "They will soon be eating rabbit gravy and bread."

Gifts of baby clothes, bought or hand-knitted, poured in. Ruth had knitted two cardigans with matching bootees and hats. Ned left them with the caretaker.

Marigold rang and invited Ruth to come and see the babies and have a cup of tea. They enjoyed this time and Marigold said, "You must come again soon."

She was kept very busy writing thank-you letters.

Maisie had knitted plenty of clothes for when they were bigger.

She told Marigold, "People always buy or knit the first size."

She replied, "Good thinking, Maisie. Thank you, darling."

Clarissa sent three beautiful Babygros for each, and a bottle of very exclusive, light, flowery perfume for Marigold.

They employed the highest-grade nannies – one for the day and one for the night.

They again invited Maisie to live with them – in her own rooms, if preferred – but she told them once more, "You need to be on your own; I have my life and friends in Cornwall. I will see you and your family when you come down. I will return to be with you again at the end of your next pregnancy."

Marigold soon regained her slim figure.

Margaret and Colin began walking when they were ten months old. When they were eleven months old, just before 6 a.m. Marigold and Jason heard voices: "Daddy. Mummy."

"The children are talking," Jason said in amazement.

Barbara, the night nanny, knocked and opened the door just wide enough for the children to come into the bedroom. They toddled across to Marigold and Jason, saying, "Daddy. Mummy."

They scooped them up into their arms and they all got back into bed to have a good cuddle.

Before long the children were able to repeat everything their parents said to them. Jason recorded them for his colleagues and the Gang. Jason rang his parents, Yvonne, Anna and Trevor as soon as they thought they would be awake. The children spoke to all of them on the mobile!

They were all thrilled of course. They had beautiful clear voices.

Jason's colleagues weren't surprised when he brought the recording; his office was covered with photographs of Marigold and the children.

After she had weaned the twins – when their teeth had come through – Marigold became pregnant again. This was deliberate; they wanted their children to grow up together.

Twins again! They were not really surprised as twins were a regular occurrence in both families.

Jason teased: "It could have been quads!"

"I wouldn't mind," Marigold told him.

"Perhaps next time?"

"I will do my best," she promised.

Twin boys were born in October. Both had fair hair. One resembled Jason's father; Philip was thrilled. The other didn't seem to resemble anyone in the family. They got all the photographs out.

"Where did he come from?" Jason teased.

"He must be from under the gooseberry bush," Marigold teased back. "He is an individual."

They were beautiful babies again; Marigold breastfed them as she had Margaret and Colin. They called them Brendan and David.

Marigold suggested to Ned, "When the animals are ready to be killed, do you think we could share our produce with the needy families in the community?"

Ned thought about this for a few minutes and advised her. "This is a tough one, Mrs Norton; they are all independent people, and they would not accept without earning."

Marigold thanked him. "I understand, Ned. Thank you for helping us as always."

Ned then told her, "The pensioners have a cooked meal in the village hall before Christmas. The Women's Institute cook it. Perhaps you could provide them with vegetables and meat for this?"

"That would be brilliant; may I leave it with you to find out what they require?"

"Yes, Mrs Norton. My wife's in that group. I'll ask her advice."

"Thanks, Ned. Whatever would we do without you! You are a star."

Ned told his pals in the pub how Mrs Norton had praised him.

They all laughed and asked, "Are you getting them all in?"

He didn't fall for that!

Jason's sports gang invited Robert, who was on leave, to make up the numbers with the lady police officers. They went for a drink afterwards. Robert and his 'partner' got on very well. They all arranged to meet up the next evening to walk the dogs on the heath, and then they had supper at the pub Jason and Marigold had introduced them to.

When Marigold heard from Jason about this, she asked, "What do you think about inviting the police officers one Sunday morning with the Gang?"

He then laughed and said, "I hope they are different from the three ladies they brought a while back."

The Gang had advised these three to bring wellingtons and anoraks, but they had complained all the time they were walking! They squealed when they were walking on slippery mud. The children had laughed, and Jason tried to tactfully stop them.

They asked Marigold, "How on earth can you like the countryside? You are a famous fashion designer and own the shop."

She assured them, "I love it and my family do. It's a healthy way of living."

During lunch they had flirted with Jason, but he pretended not to notice. His training and his ability to maintain authority with good manners were used. After lunch they all left, and Jason and Marigold took the children for their Sunday afternoon 'rest'.

"I don't think they made a good impression on the Gang," Jason said.

They hadn't, but the Gang's good manners had held. They didn't make a further date.

Jason answered Marigold's question about inviting the police officers: "Leave it to me. I'll ask Daniel first."

Daniel and all of them welcomed this. He prepared the young ladies to bring wellingtons and anoraks.

The police officers enjoyed the walk and being with the children. They were very interested in the animals, chickens and turkeys. It was a beautiful warm morning.

Marigold asked, "Please excuse me. I need to feed the babies. Please continue walking."

Pauline asked, "May we help?"

The gang laughed.

Marigold, blushing, thanked her, smiling. "I breastfeed them," she said.

"Oh, how wonderful! It gives babies the best start in life."

The gang knew this was how Marigold fed her babies from the previous time.

Robert asked, "May these little horrors stay with us?"

At that moment Kathleen fell in love with him.

Jason thanked them. The children looked happy to stay.

As they were walking a short distance away, Jason praised Marigold.

"Well done, honey! The children are secure and growing in independence. This is vital in this day and age." He made Marigold comfortable in the folding chair from under the pram.

The only sounds were the children laughing and shouting, the noises of farm animals and the birds singing, and the babies sucking hungrily.

Jason stood watching Marigold. He was filled with absolute overflowing love for her. Where would he be if he hadn't met her? Surely there must be a God in heaven. He looked round – their home bathed in sunshine, the wood, the fields filled with the animals – and he thanked God. Not for the first time he regretting having sex with women before he met Marigold, but he had been and was a virile man. Marigold kept him safe now. He still admired intelligent women and encouraged them to go further in their careers, but that was as far as it went. Everyone knew that, but to safeguard his reputation he had a male PA and he was never alone with a woman. He made sure not a breath of scandal touched him and his family.

The newspapers and magazines only reported the legal cases he was involved in; otherwise they didn't bother with him. Being happily married, he was considered too boring.

"You are deep in thought, darling. Are you sorting a problem out?"

"No, honey, I'm reflecting once again how lucky I am to have met you. I am thanking God for you, our children and all this."

"Thank you, sweetheart. You echo my gratitude."

They returned to their friends, Jason pushing the pram with one hand and with his other arm round Marigold.

"They are very much in love, aren't they?" Pauline asked.

The men agreed.

Daniel said, "They adore each other; they would be the same if they were penniless."

Adrian then told them, "They must have fallen in love at first sight."

Robert said, "Marigold's parents and grandparents left her well provided for. They bought Brierley Manor between them. They love and appreciate it here, but they would be just as happy in a small cottage. Please accept their hospitality without being embarrassed; they love to share the children, their home and grounds with friends. They aren't snobs; Marigold invites the local farmer's wife to afternoon tea so she can see the children. They are also great friends of the farmer, Ned."

Margaret chipped in, "We love Ned and Ruth."

"Oh, we had better be careful what we say now," one of them said.

They all laughed.

Robert asked, "Tell our friends about walking down to the village with your mummy to see the ducks."

Colin and Margaret both spoke at the same time about the ducks and later they drew them.

Marigold had hired the chef from the agency and two waiters to help Martin.

During lunch Jessica asked, "Are you cordon bleu, Mrs Norton?"

"Yes, I am."

Jason proudly said, "Marigold has made this bread."

They said it was so tasty. It was wonderful.

Kathleen asked, "Will you please let Robert have the recipe for us?"

"Of course I will," Marigold said gladly.

She was enjoying their company. They had beautiful manners. They asked Jason questions without flirting, and shared a brief insight into their work. Then they included Marigold, asking her about her designing. They talked with the children, who were happy with them. The men, including Robert, all looked very comfortable.

After the meal Pauline asked, "May we clear away?"

Marigold thanked them, but said she had hired extra staff.

Jason broke in with, "We are more informal with the children's supper – they help one another. We are helping them to grow up to be independent."

103

They all agreed. "You have reason to be very proud of them. They are wonderful children," said Kathleen.

Jason and Marigold thanked her.

"We are very God-blessed," Marigold said.

Jason echoed that.

Marigold took the girls to the rest rooms and left them. Later the officers set off, thanking both their hosts for a wonderful time.

"Please come again soon. You can go through the wood."

They all said they would love that. Robert went with them.

"Aren't they lovely and intelligent? They like the countryside and love sports. Kathleen and Robert seem to have hit it off," Marigold reflected to Jason.

"I am sure they are enjoying getting to know each other. I couldn't be more pleased. Thank you for making them feel so welcome. Come on – let's put the children to bed and have our Sunday afternoon rest, mm?"

She laughed. "Come on, you – but what about this morning's conversation about not being greedy?"

He came back with, "You, beautiful lady, shouldn't be so sexy."

She snuggled up to him – her precious husband and lover.

Marigold received a grateful thank-you letter from the president of the Women's Institute for her promise. Ruth agreed to co-ordinate with her nearer the time.

The president invited Marigold and the children to the meal, and asked if she would play the piano for their carol sing-song.

Marigold wrote back, accepting their kind invitation, and yes, she said she would love to play for them. She added that they were looking forward to meeting all of them.

Jason and his family were very proud of Marigold for doing this kindness.

Jason and Marigold decided to stay at Brierley Manor for Christmas. They would all share the Christmas Eve meal and Christmas Day lunch. On Boxing Day they would be going to Jason's parents' with the rest of the family. Then the family were going to Hounscliffe for the New Year. Robert was staying at Brierley Manor to help with the children.

Every Saturday morning was 'whole family time'. Jason's family came and, when possible, the twins and Robert. Jason sometimes had to work, but Marigold didn't unless there was a desperate emergency. In all weathers they went to the wood and played games with the children. When it was warm enough, they had lunch outdoors. They all adored the children.

After lunch they all left to give Jason and Marigold time alone, together and with the children.

On Mrs Holmes' recommendation, and with Martin's approval, Marigold employed a young lady cook from the village to prepare afternoon tea and the children's supper.

Lady Norton and Anna came several times during the week for afternoon tea, and they either took the children down to the village or played with them whilst Yvonne and Marigold discussed business matters.

Marigold and Jason became friendly with the local solicitor and his GP wife. Their two young children came with their nanny to play with Margaret and Colin most mornings during the week. They played together beautifully.

Margaret was always dressing and undressing her dolls, or washing them in a small bowl of water. She loved to push her little pram with her six dolls in it.

Jason said to Marigold, "It appears she is taking after your mother."

Colin loved tractors; he had a collection and loved them in books and in his bedtime stories. When the farmers' tractors were working in the fields they often took him to watch.

"Perhaps he will be a farmer," Marigold suggested.

Jason teased her: "According to Ned there is no money in farming now."

She laughed. "Well, as long as he is happy and fulfilled!"

Clarissa married her politician and they became proud parents of a daughter. Clarissa corresponded with Marigold and compared notes about their children. Her little brother was growing fast; they were all delighted with him. They were all delightful children.

Clarissa and her mum, Linda, came to Brierley Manor for afternoon tea once a week when they were free. They had a nanny to help with the children, but when they came to see Marigold they themselves brought them. Everyone looked forward to them coming, and they loved being at Brierley Manor.

Marigold never stopped her designing – outfits, wallpaper and teenage clothes. When the twins were born she had started to crochet for them, and she also made edgings for her own outfits. Yvonne suggested expanding on this line, and they employed an expert in crocheting to make edgings as well as hats and caps. Shrugs were very popular in 3-ply wool or made in silk yarn and decorated with sequins for evening wear over strapless dresses. Other fashion houses followed their lead for teenage clothes and the knitting and crocheting.

Chapter 12

Out walking, Tante asked Marigold, "Are you planning to have more children, darling?"

"Yes. I would love to have another daughter; I haven't had any trouble carrying them. Why, Tante?"

"I would like to retire and live part-time in Paris, darling. Would you like me to continue a while longer?"

"Let me talk it over with Jason, darling."

She and Jason talked at length, looking at the whole business laterally. They hadn't expected this coming yet. Then, on the following Saturday, Yvonne came for lunch so when the children were sleeping they could have a discussion.

Marigold told Tante, "I want to please you, darling, but I also have the responsibility of running Brierley, being available for the children and hopefully having more, spending time with Jason, and entertaining for him now he is in the position he is. Being responsible for the running of the design business now it has grown is a big undertaking, and it would be too much for me, darling, at least until the children are more independent."

Jason was silent. It was for them to sort out, but he stayed with them to help if he could in any way.

Yvonne admitted, "I have been feeling tired of late, darlings; the business is getting too much for me now. I will be happy to sell if that is your wish, darling Marigold. I want what is the best for you, Jason and the children. You know I adore all of you."

"We know that, Tante. After all, you have put into this business all your creativity. It has been your life – I wouldn't want to sell it. Perhaps we need to enquire about having two managers run it for us with me overseeing? I believe I could manage that." She looked at Jason.

"That happens in a lot of stores," he confirmed.

"That sounds marvellous," Yvonne agreed. "We could at least give it a try."

Marigold promised: "I will cut down on the designing – except exclusively for family and a few friends for the next few years. I want more babies."

Jason broke in: "How many more, honey? We have four."

"I would love to have another daughter for you."

"What if it's a boy again?"

"I adore the boys, but perhaps we could try again in that case."

"Blimey!" Jason laughed.

"However," Marigold said, "back to our discussion! I could continue with the teenagers because I'm not working on my own with that. I could also carry on with the wallpaper designs – that isn't too hard to do. I have been thinking for a while I would like to expand that business to include more curtains, lampshades and pottery. It is easy – not demanding."

"That's very sensible," Yvonne said. "What do you think, Jason?"

Jason said, "Excuse me, Yvonne; I'm still wondering how many more babies we are going to have."

They all laughed.

Jason and Marigold were again asked by a television 9-p.m. chat show to give them an interview. They agreed.

They sat on a settee holding hands and answered all the questions. Photographs were shown of their two homes and grounds.

It was a great success. They were both relaxed and their personalities shone through. Jason projected his charm and sexiness.

The presenter asked an unexpected question: "You and Mrs Norton did not live together when you went to Hounscliffe?"

Marigold blushed. Jason looked annoyed.

"No, we did not," he said.

From his tone the presenter knew to leave it there. He quickly came in with, "Are you hoping to have lots more children?"

Jason and Marigold laughed. "We are."

Everyone knew they adored each other.

They were asked to give magazine interviews. They agreed only if they could see the proofs before printing!

Whilst Jason and Marigold were out walking with Nelson, Jason said, "Honey, I have never been into religion and that kind of thing; I have always been in awe of the beauty of the earth, but I have been thinking lately that there must be a God. How you and I met when I almost didn't go to that party; how you were hurt at the beginning but overcame – there must be someone looking after us."

With tears in her eyes, Marigold replied, "I have always believed, Jason. For years I couldn't understand why my family and others were killed, but I have to accept that these things happen because of human fragilities."

"Yes, darling, it was a drunken driver in your family's case."

They walked in silence, deep in thought. They had never had such an in-depth conversation before, but they knew with certainty they were soulmates.

A few days later, Marigold told Jason as they were soaking in their bath, "I am feeling broody, darling."

Jason asked, "Is your body ready?"

"Yes it is."

He jumped out of the bath and helped her out! "What are we waiting for?"

She laughed with joy.

Jason mentioned to Ned, "We need a chauffeur now."

Ned told him about a decent family man, a fireman who had recently married a local schoolteacher. "She is fed up with him being called out in the night on emergencies; then she can't sleep for worrying. She knew before they married that he got called out, but she hadn't known how often. He hasn't left the fire service yet, but it is the talk at the pub that he is looking for a new job."

"He sounds promising; will you ask him to ring me, please?"

Ned was proud to be doing this errand. He went to Paul's before going into the pub.

Paul rang Jason and they arranged to meet. Jason was a good

judge of character, and he saw that Paul was a decent man. Paul, being a fireman, already had a police check and regular health checks.

"I need someone to take me to work, run Mrs Norton about, clean the two cars and yard and fetch me home."

Paul mentioned, "Temporarily the fire service has asked me to work afternoons 2 till 5, sir, cleaning the fire engines and yard and being on standby. They are building a larger station, about two miles away in the new community. Our station will close down. If you want me to work full-time for you and Mrs Norton, then I will, please, sir."

"That's fine, Paul. In the meantime, then, you work for us in the mornings, Monday to Friday. Come at 8 a.m. and run me to work. Then take Mrs Norton and Miss Grafton with the children to the nursery, Monday, Wednesday and Friday. On Wednesday morning, go on Mrs Norton's shop, wait and return them to pick the children up at 12. On some of the free mornings, Mrs Norton will need to go to the doctor's for check-ups. Also, there will be appointments for the dentist, etc. Otherwise use these free mornings to clean the cars and yard. How does that sound, Paul?"

"Thank you, sir. This should work out well."

"Good man! Now wage – how much do you want?"

Paul told him.

"Yes, that's satisfactory."

Paul then suggested, "If you agree, sir, I could work on Saturday mornings 8 till 1 to clean your cars if I haven't had time during the week. Also, if Mrs Norton agrees, I could clean your windows and paintwork. Whilst I am up the ladders I could clean your guttering out as well. With my fireman training, I have no fear of climbing ladders."

"Thank you, Paul. I'll ask Mrs Norton and let you know."

Marigold was pleased. "This sounds all right; the window cleaners don't always turn up. I'll let them know."

The window cleaners knew Paul and his situation, so there was no hard feelings between them. One of them told him, "Really, Paul, Brierley has been too much for us to do with our other commitments. You'll never get all the windows done in one morning!"

He laughed and said, "I will do what I can in the time, then next time I'll start again where I left off."

Yvonne came for lunch again the following Saturday. She had had good encouraging news of very experienced women who had applied to be the manager of the shop.

Marigold shared with her, "I'm hoping I am pregnant."

Yvonne said, "They are so lucky having you as parents – your lovely family, this beautiful home and Hounscliffe!"

"We are truly God-blessed, aren't we, Tante? We have all that as well as having you."

Yvonne began crying. Marigold and Jason were shocked.

"I am sorry; I did warn you that I am feeling tired."

"Have you had a check-up, Tante?" asked Marigold.

"No."

Jason went to the cellar and brought back a bottle of their very best red wine. He poured them a glass each and put Yvonne's feet up on the stool.

Marigold said firmly, "You must make an appointment on Monday, or should I now contact a private doctor? You are probably anaemic."

"Leave it until Monday, darling."

Marigold promised, "I will take you."

Jason then firmly said, "You must stay here with us, Yvonne, for a few days. We will fetch the clothes you need."

With tears in her eyes, Marigold nodded. "Yes. Please, Tante, stay with us here, where we can feed you up and make you rest."

"Thank you," Yvonne said. "I don't want to be in the way."

"Dearest Tante, you didn't hesitate about taking Nanny and me in when our family was killed. You know I have always wanted you to live here with us. I will go and tell Mrs Holmes to have rooms prepared for you. Do you want to be at the front or back?"

"I don't mind, darling; all the views are so lovely here."

Marigold went and arranged that. Jason gave Yvonne another glass of the wine before he went up to tell the nanny. "We may be delayed a little while. Please bring the children down when they wake," he said.

"Certainly I will, sir."

When he returned, Yvonne had fallen into a deep sleep. He

went to tell Marigold to leave her there. They went up to the nursery and helped to get the children ready for tea.

On Monday morning Marigold left her colleagues working whilst she took Yvonne to the doctor. He looked closely at her and took her blood pressure and a sample of blood. Her blood pressure was high.

"Make an appointment for tomorrow afternoon; I will then have the results of the blood test," he said, smiling at Marigold. He sternly said to Yvonne, "You, young lady, have not been looking after yourself. It's all right trying to hide how you are feeling with make-up, but you cannot go on for ever."

Marigold thanked him for seeing them.

As they were travelling home, Marigold said, "Darling Tante, you are definitely staying with us. Please don't argue. I am so ashamed at not noticing you are tired."

"As the doctor observed, I have disguised my ill health with make-up. Make-up covers a multitude of sins." Yvonne laughed.

Marigold had asked Martin to make nourishing soup for lunch. She made sure Tante ate plenty. She ordered her to bed for the afternoon. Yvonne's PA kept the shop ticking over. Everyone was so sorry that Yvonne was ill, and she received lots of good wishes for her full recovery.

When they returned to the doctor for the result of the blood test, he looked serious. "There is bad news and good news," he told them.

"Yes, what is it?" Marigold asked.

"I regret it's leukaemia, but the good news is we have caught it in the early stages. It can be treated, but your lifestyle must change dramatically. You must give up most of your commitments with the shop."

"Yes," Yvonne said, "Mrs Norton and I have been in discussion this last week about our business. My niece is busy with her home and family of course, but I am going to retire and we will have managers in."

"This is good timing," he agreed. "I am sorry it is bad news, but, as I said, with treatment and rest you will get stronger."

When Marigold shook his hand after Tante, he gave Marigold a serious look.

She nodded. She understood that it was quite serious.

She remained strong until after she had reached home and she had taken Yvonne up to her room to sleep. Then she went downstairs into their lounge and wept broken-heartedly. Mrs Holmes came looking for her, to ask if she wanted a cup of tea. She was very disturbed to find her crying so.

Marigold dried her eyes and explained: "Tante has leukaemia, Mrs Holmes. We needn't tell people until she is stronger with the medication."

"No, ma'am. I'll bring you a pot of tea."

"Thank you. I will go up to the nursery – please have it sent there."

Jason rang her to find out what the doctor had said.

Marigold asked, "May I text you?"

"Of course, honey. I will be with you soon."

Marigold did, however, tell the children's nanny. With her experience of nursing, she understood. She was so sorry to hear the alarming news, but she knew that with catching it in time there was hope. She commiserated with Marigold.

"Thank you, Nanny."

The children then woke up.

After a few weeks, when Yvonne was stronger, she went to friends in Spain for the warmer climate. She was soon feeling so much better, being near the sea. The shop was running with oiled wheels with the expertise of the new managers and Marigold overseeing.

Chapter 13

Maisie came back up, jokingly asking, "How many more times?"

Marigold gave birth to the twins, both boys, both healthy. Roland had black curls and blue eyes; Malcolm was fair with the look of Colin. Everyone was delighted.

Marigold joked, "I aim to please."

As before, gifts of baby clothes and toys were given.

Jason said to Marigold, "That's it now, honey – no more! Three sets of twins are enough for your body."

"I would love to have just one more pregnancy to provide another daughter for you, darling."

"We have Margaret, and I adore the little boys."

"I know you do. So do I. We are very God-blessed, aren't we?"

Jason had a talk with the private doctor, Michael, about a further pregnancy.

Michael assured him, "There should be no problem. Mrs Norton has a very healthy womb, and with her keeping fit and her good diet, plus breastfeeding the babies, which helps to heal the womb, I cannot see any problem. Perhaps you had better wait for eighteen months or so. Do you want me to put Mrs Norton on the pill?"

"No, thank you, Michael; I will take care of her. Thank you for telling me Marigold is in good health."

Unfortunately, two months later Yvonne had a turn for the worse. Jason and a private nurse fetched her home to Brierley Manor. She stayed in bed, sleeping most of the time, but they, Lady Norton, Anna and personal friends of Yvonne's took it in turns to sit with her.

The nurse found Marigold early one morning and told her, "I am sorry, Mrs Norton – your aunt has passed away peacefully in her sleep."

Tributes from all the fashion houses poured in for Yvonne. The church was packed to overflowing for the funeral; speakers were put outside so that the crowds could follow the service. Marigold and the whole family were devastated by the quick ending of Yvonne's life.

Marigold received hundreds of messages encouraging her to continue the business.

Jason went to see his parents; Roland and Malcolm were three months old now. Marigold was still breastfeeding them, as she had the other babies.

He suggested, "I don't want to put too much work on Marigold's shoulders, but I would like all of us to go to Hounscliffe for three weeks' holiday. It will help her in her grieving for Yvonne. I realise it will be a mammoth operation, but if we all work together and plan, it should go smoothly without any of us being burdened."

They agreed.

"We will do everything to help – you know that, Jason," said his mother.

"Right, I will now have a word with Marigold and we will work out when we can go. Late July, or the beginning of August, will be my best time."

"I will check my diary and consult my team; there are plenty to take over for me," Sir Philip said. "I have been thinking for a while that it is time to wind down ready for retirement."

"I agree, Dad. OK, I will discuss this with Marigold, but I think our best plan would be to travel by car with both of you to help us with the children. We could hire a suitable vehicle and possibly Joseph will drive us. If we stop off at a hotel en route for a meal, Marigold will be able to feed the twins in comfort."

"You have been giving this much careful thought, Jason. If Joseph drives, we can stop when the children tire or want to use their potties. The twins might also come – and Robert if he can get a bit of leave – but they can travel by train with their sports gear."

"Thanks, Dad, Mum. I'll be in touch soon. Please let me know when you can have leave, Dad."

That Saturday afternoon Jason and Marigold went walking in their grounds. The children were all sleeping. They left them in the capable hands of the nannies, Dianne and Brenda.

"Honey, I would like all of us to go to Hounscliffe for two or three weeks. It will do you the world of good. I realise it will take some planning, but we will all work together so no one will be overstressed."

"I think this is a brilliant idea, darling. We must ask Dad and Mum."

"I have had a preliminary word with them and I have asked when Dad can get leave," Jason assured her.

"We must now make sure Aunt Anna and Trevor are available."

Susan had already done this, and there was no problem – Trevor would clear this time with his partners. Philip had faxed Robert and the twins.

"I suggested to Dad and Mum that we hire a big car. Joseph and I can do the driving. My parents could travel with us to help with the children. We can book in for a meal at the hotel where we stopped and had afternoon tea when we travelled back that Sunday afternoon."

"That would be a perfect place to stop off," Marigold agreed. "We will all be able to stretch our legs in their lovely grounds. I will be able to feed the twins in comfort and make the others comfortable. Anna and Trevor could travel with us if the car is big enough."

"I was thinking that the twins and Robert (if he can come) would go down on the express train with all their sports kits, but it would be better if all of us could travel together. How can we work this out?"

"What about two separate cars?"

"What about a luxury coach?" Jason suggested.

"That's a great idea, but we wouldn't be able to stop if there was a problem with the children. It will be their first long ride."

"Good point, honey! If you have to feed the twins en route, and the children need their potty, we will all be more comfortable going by car. When they are older we can certainly go in the express train. The children will love that."

"They will, darling."

"Let's discuss this with Trev. Do you want the nannies to come with us, honey?"

"No, let them have a holiday; we will be more relaxed just with family."

"We can all help you. Everybody will enjoy that, including the children, and as we are on holiday we will be able to give 100%."

"We need to make lists and compare with everyone."

"That's good thinking, Marigold."

Marigold made a list of furniture and what they would need for the children and the babies. It was a long list, but once they had everything in at Hounscliffe it wouldn't be as hard for future holidays. She showed Jason.

He said, "Wow! Yes, we will need all these."

Marigold gave Susan and Anna this list; they left an order with a London store and asked them to deliver to Hounscliffe everything from cots and pushchairs to nappies and a special soap powder!

Martin promised to cook for them. Marigold invited him to stay with them, but he asked if he could stay at the Rock Hotel.

"Of course, Martin. If that is what you prefer, we will cover all your bills."

"I will drive myself down, Mrs Norton, so if I can take anything or anyone with me, please let me know."

Marigold discussed this with Trevor and Anna. They said they would be delighted if Martin was happy to take them with him. Trevor offered to drive part of the way, and Martin was happy with this arrangement.

"It's a long way on your own. Thank you, Mrs Norton, for that thought."

Nathan, Peter and their friends Dominic and Stephen booked seats on the train.

Lord and Lady Sutton (Walter and Rachel), now they knew Susan and Philip would be there, were going to their holiday home for the same period, taking their chef and housekeeper.

Robert arranged to follow a few days later by train also.

"Everything is taking shape, honey," Jason remarked.

"Yes, sweetheart, it's wonderful. Everyone is working together."

They carefully enquired and hired a luxury car with plenty of seats; Joseph and Jason had a practice run in it. Joseph was a first-class driver. They could trust him to take them down without speeding, and he agreed to stop in a lay-by whenever they needed him to.

He asked, "Am I required during your holiday, sir?"

Philip asked him, "Would you like to be? You would be welcome."

Joseph told him, "I would like to holiday with my brother and sister-in-law. They have offered to rent a holiday bungalow with me for the three weeks. They will collect me from Hounscliffe, and then bring me back to take you home."

"You could stay with us, Joseph," Jason invited.

"Thank you, sir. I know, but I would like to take this opportunity to be with my family and friends."

"Our staff don't want to stay with us," Jason later teased Marigold. "We must be frightening."

"No, it isn't that, darling: they are afraid of being overfamiliar."

"Well," laughed Jason, "they would be embarrassed if they met us in the middle of the night in their pyjama bottoms."

"How do you know they wear pyjamas?" she laughed back.

"I don't, but meeting them without would be even more disastrous!"

"I think planning this holiday is exciting you too much!"

"Where will the children sleep?" Jason asked.

"I thought Roland and Malcolm would be with us, of course, for me to feed them. Margaret, Colin, Brendan and David would be in the next room with a baby monitor."

"Have you ordered one?"

"Yes – two!"

Susan asked if she and Philip could have the room next to the children with a monitor in their room, so Marigold could sleep uninterruptedly between the feeds. They welcomed this.

Marigold thanked them for everything. She said, "It's going to be a marvellous holiday. I am sorry Tante isn't with us." She burst out crying.

Jason pulled her on to his knee and stroked her hair.

Jason and Marigold's friends Bill the solicitor and Mary his GP wife would have loved to spend some of the holiday with them, but they had arranged to go with their family to Turkey.

Marigold reassured them: "There is always next year. The children will love playing together."

In Cornwall, the local organic farm shop delivered fresh supplies every morning, including bread, freshly caught fish, and fruit. They received orders from across the community.

Nathan and Peter fetched Maisie up for the day every morning. She sat knitting and played and helped with the children. They loved her and called her 'Nanny-Nanny'.

Nathan, Peter and Robert also stayed with the family every morning. They all helped with the children in the rock pools, made sandcastles or played games at Harlyn Bay. Then after lunch they joined Dominic and Stephen to surf, windsurf or play sport, either at Harlyn Bay, Watergate Bay, Porthtowan or Fistral Beach. Robert came back for dinner, but Nathan and Peter either ate with Walter and Rachel or went to a place of their own choice with Dominic and Stephen. Marigold invited them to come to Hounscliffe for dinner, but they said they would be too noisy and disturb the children sleeping. Jason and Marigold were overwhelmed by this mature thought.

After dinner the family washed up. Martin's time was his own until it was time for him to cook breakfast for them. He quickly made friends with the bar staff and waiters at the Rock Hotel. Marigold felt much happier when he told them this. In fact he enjoyed himself so much that he booked his holidays at the Rock Hotel for next year.

The children and babies woke up at about 6 a.m. They had settled well in their unfamiliar rooms.

Sir Philip stated, "This proves they are secure. They know they are loved and safe and with you both encouraging them to take small risks in their playing."

All the men but Jason went swimming at this time. They were all so pleased there was now a pool at Hounscliffe.

"Darling, please go with them," Marigold said. "You know I want you to be with us, but it is your holiday too and you haven't had much opportunity to spend time with your brothers."

"What about bathing the children?" he asked.

"Your mum, Anna and I will manage with Margaret and Colin's help. Some young mothers have more to cope with than I have in the mornings."

"Does that mean we can do without the day nannies?"

"We could manage without a nanny at night!"

"Now that I most certainly say no to," Jason replied. He grabbed her and they kissed passionately. "Right, I'll go for a swim. Thank you, sweetheart. Whatever have I done to deserve a wife like you?"

"Don't overdo it, darling," she teased.

The men were amazed to see Jason join them. He told them what Marigold had said. "Isn't she brilliant!" he exclaimed.

They all acknowledged that.

After dinner Marigold and Jason had a swim at 9.30, and then soaked in their big bath. The family made sure they were free for this time.

The wonderful hot weather held.

Whilst the children slept after lunch, Maisie, Susan, Philip, Anna and Trevor had a rest in the lounge with the baby monitors set. Jason and Marigold walked with Nelson in the wood.

Then they all went for a countryside run in the large hired car with Jason driving.

On Monday, Wednesday and Friday they called at the friendly café near Geoff's for afternoon tea and Cornish ice cream.

Marigold fed the babies in privacy in the stockroom. Maisie went with her. It was spotlessly clean but cluttered!

The waitresses loved them (especially the children) to come. They put tables shaded by big umbrellas out in the garden for them.

They picked Betty up on Wednesday afternoons. She always nearly swooned when she saw Jason! They all loved her; she was marvellous with the children. To help her business, Marigold bought rolls of material from her for her personal use. Betty now knew what Marigold liked. Maisie and her friends went regularly to her shop to buy all their wool.

They also called at Potter's to let Mrs Haslam and Cheryl see the children. Susan and Anna often bought something from the shop.

Philip, Susan, Anna and Trevor went to their friends Walter and Rachel for dinner twice a week, and they came to them at Houncliffe regularly.

The children loved it; there were plenty of tractors for Colin to watch. He was always drawing, and when they stopped he drew the tractors and fields.

Margaret still adored her dolls – washing and dressing them, and combing their hair. She also liked to comb the grown-ups' hair.

Maisie told them, "Marigold loved brushing my hair."

Margaret and Colin were both keen readers and they played games which involved spelling. Margaret had activity books in which there were dolls' clothes to colour and cut out to match the dolls illustrated. Dominic loved cars. David preferred aeroplanes. He watched them in the sky. They all squabbled, but they were left alone to sort themselves out. They were really very good friends and kind to one another. Everybody loved them. Margaret was a beauty – very graceful. At home she had started half-hour ballet lessons. She could wind Jason round her little finger, but he and everyone treated all the children the same.

They loved the baby twins and splashed them whilst they were being bathed. The babies chuckled.

Marigold and Jason thanked God every day for all their blessings.

The holiday passed too quickly, but, as Susan said, "Now we have the children's equipment set up, we can have weekends in the good weather."

Back home, Marigold only accepted a few orders for outfits; she did this work in the afternoons whilst the children slept. Wallpaper designing was no problem; the producers incorporated the same designs in lampshades and pottery. These were a great success. She continued with her designs for teenagers and also passed on her designs for washable children's clothes based on what her children were comfortable in.

On most afternoons, Susan and Anna came for afternoon tea, and they walked with the children down to the village or through the new kitchen garden and the fields where the cows, sheep and horses were. Marigold often invited Ruth.

Jason was working hard to be a Queen's Counsel. Marigold entertained his colleagues, politicians and senior police. They all encouraged him.

As Marigold was still breastfeeding the babies, she and Jason didn't accept return invitations, but she promised they would after she had weaned the babies.

Everyone loved coming to Brierley Manor. They were disappointed when they didn't have rabbit and Marigold's home-made bread. They all enjoyed the musical times, in which they all took part, and they loved to walk on the horseshoe walk in the light from the lamps.

Susan, Philip, Anna and Trevor came when they were free.

The professionals recognised that Jason had all the qualities to be a judge, especially his ability to absorb and analyse information quickly. He had a first-class brain and a thorough knowledge of law and its underlying principles, or the ability to acquire this knowledge where necessary. Also he had integrity and independence of mind, sound judgement, and the ability and willingness to learn.

They also grew to know Marigold and appreciate her integrity; they saw how she supported her husband and they knew she would keep him safe in his career. Marigold knew Jason worked daily with beautiful, charismatic, intelligent women, but she never had any fear that he would be unfaithful to her. She trusted him and knew he would never ever hurt her and the children.

The weekend night nanny, Helen, was also highly qualified. She came from the agency. On Saturdays and Sundays she went home after helping at breakfast with Sylvia, a trainee nanny.

On Saturday mornings the family came, but Jason often had to work and occasionally Marigold had to see one of her few customers. This might occur because the customer worked all the week and Saturday was the only time they could both manage.

They all walked through the wood with the babies in their pram, and played games with the children. A lady cook from the village helped Martin to cook lunch. After helping with the children, the family went home.

Jason and Marigold put the children to bed for their afternoon nap. They had a rest before taking the children to the pool for a 'swim' in the shallow end. They bathed Roland and Malcolm and gave them their supper. Margaret, Colin and Brendan and David helped. After putting them in their cots and bed, Jason and Marigold read them a story each.

Helen and Sylvia came at 8 p.m.

Chapter 14

When Malcolm and Roland were eighteen months old Marigold became pregnant again. Jason had been worried, but he didn't let anyone see it and he remembered the doctor's words about her being healthy. He didn't want Marigold to have any regrets about not having another daughter. She suffered more morning sickness this time. The scan showed twins again.

When they were alone, Marigold said to Jason, "I think you are unhappy about this pregnancy." She was intelligent and he couldn't hide from her that something was wrong.

He started crying.

She was shocked. She had never seen him cry. She sat on his lap and cuddled him close.

"Jason, my precious, please be happy for me. I am so thankful to be having these babies. I promise you I will take care of myself, but, please, I do not want you or anyone else wrapping me up in cotton wool."

"It's definitely snip time after this."

"Are you sure? Next time it could be quads!" she teased.

He groaned. "I think eight will be enough for us to manage." He began to feel positive again.

Marigold held him close, knowing strong emotions were going through him and that he was getting rid of his worries.

Jason asked Michael, their private doctor, to tell him the scan results.

"You will have two daughters."

Jason began to feel better for Marigold's sake, but he resolved that this would be the last time. No more – definitely! Even if

Marigold protested, he was having the snip! Eight children! He laughed to himself. Eight children! Thankfully, they would have enough money to see them all through university if they so wished.

Marigold and the children, Jason, their family and friends walked round the garden and wood, but Jason didn't let Marigold go through the rough fields when it was muddy. She began to design more flamboyantly; her customers, particularly the film stars, loved this new look. She went to garden centres, looking for vibrantly coloured flowering plants and buying them for the greenhouse, and she sent away for the seeds of exotic flowers for the gardeners to grow. As well as plants, flowers and seeds Marigold also received hundreds of photographs of unusual flowers and plants. Some came from Cornwall. Her PA acknowledged every one and said how grateful Marigold was. Jason, his gang and colleagues bought colourful plants and flowers also.

Marigold photographed the flowers and used them as a basis for her fabric and wallpaper designs. They were bolder designs than before, often incorporating some large and some small flowers. She mixed and matched. Everyone was delighted.

She designed more very fashionable hats. The milliners couldn't keep pace with demand.

She also kept mixing bread and had a lady personal trainer come.

Marigold had always looked her best for Jason, but she now took even more pride in her hair. Gillian came on Monday afternoons as usual, her senior assistant came on Thursday mornings and a beautician came to massage her body with special moisturising oils and wax her legs.

She spent time with her children as always. They all kept rubbing her stomach lovingly. They were looking forward to the babies. Everyone was. Even if one or both didn't resemble Marigold, it wouldn't matter. All Jason wanted was for her to be well and the children healthy.

The scans showed the twins were growing healthily. Marigold again didn't ask the sexes.

The children with Jason went up to the third storey of Brierley Manor and brought their old toys down for the new babies. They saved their pocket money and bought toys and books.

Marigold and Jason swam carefully. He was most tender with her, making her feel very precious. He bought her special moisturising creams, hand creams and hair beauty treatments. She had taken a dislike to strong coffee, so he bought her mild coffee beans.

He asked her shop to make her some glamorous nightdresses. They knew this was because of her increased interest in wanting to look her best.

They still made gentle love. Jason wanted to wait, but Marigold said she needed this; she adored him so much.

Maisie came up when Marigold was only three months pregnant. There was no concern, but she wanted to be near her.

When she arrived, she greeted Marigold with, "Surely this will be the last time I come for babies!"

They all laughed.

"You look well, darling," she said to Marigold.

"Thank you, Nanny. I am amazingly well."

Maisie privately asked Marigold, "Do you know the sexes?"

"No. I like to be surprised."

"Does the pregnancy feel different this time?"

"Yes: I am not as big. I have a great appetite for vibrancy, Nanny; I need to be surrounded by vibrant colours."

"That's all right, darling. Everyone is so pleased with this and how you are expressing it in your talents."

"I hope it doesn't leave me when the babies are born."

"No, I am sure it will not. You are maturing now, darling, and your creativity is coming to full fruition. Have you any photographs of hats you have recently designed?"

Marigold showed her.

"These are beautiful. They are too young for me, but I can see why they are so popular."

Marigold showed her the hats she had made for Margaret – beautiful hats decorated with ribbons and small hand-made flowers.

"Margaret must love these."

"She does. I will design two hats for you, darling Nanny. What colours would you like?"

Later, whilst Marigold was resting, Maisie and Jason went for a walk by themselves.

"How is she, Maisie?"

"She is fine, Jason – no problems. I would imagine she is carrying two girls, yes?"

"Yes," he replied. "Please don't tell her I know the sexes, will you?"

"Of course not. I thought you knew me better than that!"

"I do, Maisie. Sorry. As soon as she is able to travel we will all come down to Hounscliffe."

"That's good."

The scans were satisfactory. The babies were very active, especially when Marigold was swimming or soaking in the big bath with Jason.

Chapter 15

When she was in the sixth month of her pregnancy Marigold received a fax from Grace, one of Tante's colleagues. She said she hoped Marigold and the babies were well. She was retiring, and she wondered if Marigold would like to buy her shop in Mayfair. The shop sold men's and ladies' ready-made wear, haberdashery and textiles. It was a busy and highly respected shop.

Marigold faxed her back: 'We are all well. Thank you for letting me know about your retirement. May I think about your business and talk it over with Jason? Please let me have full details of space. I am interested; I will be in touch very soon.'

Grace faxed her: 'Of course, darling.'

Marigold had been thinking for a while that her shop needed larger premises as it had grown so much over the last few years. It seemed as though Grace's shop could be just what she was looking for. She discussed it with Jason and Trevor, her financial adviser.

Enquiries were made. Grace's business was very sound and had a marvellous yearly turnover. The shop needed updating, but it was larger than Marigold's. She cried because Tante and her mother weren't there to advise her and be part of this.

Jason took her to see Grace's shop from the outside. The window displays radiated elegance and quality.

Jason had booked a table at the hotel they had used for their engagement and wedding parties. The manager and staff welcomed them very warmly, and they were given the best-positioned table.

Jason and Marigold talked.

He told her, "The decision is yours, honey."

"I have been having thoughts lately about moving to larger premises."

"Then go for it, honey darling. You will be able to get another manager, won't you?"

"No problem, but I couldn't close Grace's business. It is too popular and trustworthy after all her years there building it up and gaining a reputation for quality. Possibly I could move the hats and gloves there," she mused. "It really is too good an opportunity to miss, sweetheart."

As they travelled back home, Marigold told him, "Although Tante and Mummy aren't here, as a tribute to them I will make this new venture a success."

Marigold telephoned Grace early next morning: "After discussing this with Jason, I will be very pleased to buy your shop."

Grace was delighted to know that her lifetime work was going into good hands. She hadn't daughters; she had three sons but, even though they and their wives and children loved her, they were not interested in the fashion business.

Marigold met with her two managers to tell them of this new venture. She told them the shop would remain largely as it is, but perhaps they would move the hats and gloves there.

The managers were both very excited about this, and their enthusiasm confirmed Marigold's thoughts about moving to larger premises. Mayfair was a wonderful area to be in and she saw the takeover as a great opportunity. She told them about her determination to make this new venture a success in memory of her mother and aunt.

"We are with you 100%, Mrs Norton."

"Thank you. I know you are. And I again tell you both how grateful I am to you for all your help – especially whilst I carry the babies."

They laughed. "We are never surprised when you let us know you are expecting. We know you and Mr Norton desire a large family."

Marigold laughed. "This is the last time."

"The others are beautiful children, and these two will be as precious."

Marigold agreed and thanked them. "Now, back to business," she said: "I am giving you both a rise in salary."

They both protested: "There is no need, Mrs Norton. In fact, if we could manage without the money, we would do the job for love."

They all laughed.

Grace faxed Marigold's PA: 'Please ask Mrs Norton to ring me as soon as possible.'

Marigold rang her, thinking something was wrong with the proposed sale.

"Darling Marigold, I have some news you may be interested in."

Marigold laughed. "Good!"

"May we meet up?"

"Yes, of course, Grace. Could you get to Brierley? I have been on my feet all morning, so I am relaxing this afternoon as usual with my younger children."

"I will be with you at 2.30 if this is OK."

"Perfect, Grace! See you then. The children will be noisy, but they always are when they play with their toys."

"I will love being with them."

Marigold faxed Jason about this meeting.

When Grace was settled with a coffee, after greeting the children, she began: "I told Patrick, the young hairdresser next-door, of my retiring and selling-up. I didn't tell him you were the buyer, only that I might have an interested party."

Marigold listened intently.

"He is getting married, darling, and of course they need to set up home. He has already been struggling with the mortgage on his shop. You will appreciate it is in a most prestigious area, so property is pricey. After I told him, he said he would put his shop up for sale also and move to smaller, more affordable, premises. I asked him to hold that thought and said that if he would give me space, I might be able to help him with the sale."

"Actually, Grace, Jason took me out for dinner last night and we stopped to look at your shop. Jason teased me by saying that ownership of the hairdresser and beauty shop would enable the business to grow even more! We could leave your shop as it is in that case, Grace." She continued: "I am definitely interested. May I talk it over with Jason? Will I need planning permission or anything for the change?"

"I hadn't thought about that, darling."

"Jason will know, or he will be able to find out from his colleagues."

"Of course Jason will find out, darling Marigold. I wish you were my daughter."

"Thank you, Grace. Now we have more contact I would like you to keep in touch with my family and me. Would you like a drink, darling?"

"A glass of red wine will be good. What about you, Marigold? Are you able to have alcohol?"

"A small glass, Grace; but I mostly drink water."

She rang for Mrs Holmes.

After their drink they changed their shoes and took the children for a stroll. As they walked they chatted about the fashion business.

Grace told her, "My staff is hoping to be retained. They are professionals."

"I trust your recommendation, Grace. I am grateful for any help. I need to spend time with my growing family and of course my precious husband."

"Avril, my younger personal assistant, is interested in applying to be your manager, Marigold. She is highly proficient. She is a widow with no children, so her job is now her life. She will help you take your business further."

"Thank you for this, Grace. I recognised her expertise six years ago at my first October show. Will you tell her, please?"

"I will also help you, darling Marigold. Yvonne would be so proud of you."

"Thank you, Grace," Marigold said with tears in her eyes.

Marigold hosted a celebration lunch at Brierley Manor the following Saturday for Grace and her personal assistants, and

Marigold's two managers. Susan, Philip, Anna, Trevor and Robert came of course. They kept the conversation social and everyone was encouraged to participate.

Grace's assistants and Marigold's managers left after thanking her and Jason for the wonderful lunch and their hospitality. Jason had ordered a taxi to bring them and take them back to the shops, so they had been able to have a glass or two of wine with their meal. Grace, by arrangement with Marigold, stayed on.

Jason and the family went to join the children and take them to play on the lawn, waiting for Marigold and Grace.

Grace thanked Marigold for the lunch and for buying her shop. She said she could retire in peace, knowing it would be in good hands. Grace then asked, "Do you want to stretch your legs, darling?"

"Yes please, Grace."

When they stood up, Grace took her into her arms. She knew Marigold was near to tears in this emotional time.

"Come on, darling – let's find your handsome husband."

Marigold then went upstairs for a rest.

The children all changed their shoes to take Grace for a walk through the gardens and fields to show her the animals. She had asked if this was possible.

Marigold joined them for afternoon tea. It was a happy time. The children told their mother about the animals and how many eggs they had collected. They had taken some photographs to show her. Jason fetched Grace a dozen eggs to take home.

As Susan, Philip, Anna and Trevor were taking Grace home, she said, "I am so thankful it's Marigold who has bought my business. I can now retire in peace. If needed, I have promised Marigold I will help her in any way I can, with her being in the last stage of her pregnancy."

They told her how grateful they were for this.

Marigold went to view Patrick's with Philip, Susan, Anna and Trevor. They were all wowed by the shop. It was in a very good position, and it had four large windows, ideal for display. They were all happy about this.

Trevor advised Marigold: "You are investing your savings very wisely."

There was a car-parking area not far away. It was a very select area.

Mr Rudd, the estate agent, had told her about the rooms at the back, which were currently being used for beauty treatments and massage. She was pleased when she saw these. The space could be made into excellent changing rooms as well as rest rooms with more toilets and facilities for redoing make-up and hair – vital in the fashion business.

She asked Mr Rudd, "Is planning permission needed for this work?"

He promised to check.

Marigold asked Patrick to leave a washbasin in the area which would be the shop. Toilets and other facilities would be put upstairs.

Marigold asked Patrick, "May I bring my husband this evening?"

"I would be very delighted, Mrs Norton."

Two photographers were waiting for Marigold as she came out. She said good morning and moved on. They followed.

"Are you buying this, Mrs Norton?"

She just smiled.

They then asked, "Please give us a break!"

She knew they were only doing their job – and they had left her and Jason alone lately.

"I am interested. How did you know I was here?"

"We spotted you in the car and followed."

She laughed. "I'll keep you informed."

They photographed her and the family. Patrick was stood in the doorway smiling.

She rang Jason. His mobile wasn't switched on, so she knew he was busy, but she left him a message: "Darling, may I take you out this evening on a date? Can you possibly get home early?"

Philip asked, "Would you like to go anywhere else whilst we are in this area, Marigold?"

She thanked him. "Shall we go and see the other shops that are here?"

They all agreed.

Mr Rudd had already told her what was on the road.

They stopped at a shoe shop, where Marigold spotted Italian leather sandals.

"May we go in?" she asked.

"Of course, darling – whatever you want to do."

She bought a pair of the sandals and kept them on – they were so comfortable!

"I'll bring my children next time," she promised.

Susan and Anna asked the assistant if they had their size sandals in. They hadn't, but they promised to get them for the following day.

Philip asked, "Anywhere else?"

Marigold thanked him. "I would now like to get back to the children before Margaret and Colin return to school for their afternoon lessons."

When they got back home, the two children were setting off. Marigold gathered them into her arms.

"Have a lovely afternoon, darlings. I will be here when you come home."

"OK, Mummy," they both said. "Bye."

Dianne went with them.

"I don't think they have missed me," Marigold laughed. "It's good that they feel secure."

She later thanked Dianne, Anna and Maisie for the morning.

"They were fine," Anna told her. "In fact, they were proud to tell their teacher that their mother is buying a new shop. You have no secrets now! Then they showed their friends the photographs of the animals."

David, Dominic, Malcolm and Roland all rushed out to meet her. She cuddled them.

They went in for a late lunch before Marigold went to her room for a rest. Maisie went with her to 'tuck her in'. She immediately went into a deep sleep. Maisie went back down to the family.

After Marigold woke, Jason rang her back: "Thank you for the promise of a date. Yes, my colleagues are helping to enable me to be home early. Love you, honey."

When Paul fetched him, Jason asked him, "Make sure the car is topped up as Mrs Norton and I are going out this evening."

Marigold had booked a table at the pub she and Jason went to when they first met.

The local fire station had now shut down, and the fire service operated from a larger station two miles away, where a new community had been built – as Paul had mentioned when he first came to Brierley Manor. He had been made redundant, so he now worked full-time for Jason and Marigold. This was useful for his whole family. Paul's colleagues had been offered jobs at the new station.

On the way to the pub, Jason and Marigold called at the hairdresser's in Mayfair. They went in and she introduced Patrick. Jason was impressed by the size of the property and he liked the upstairs rooms.

"There is plenty of good light," he said.

"Yes, that is vital in a fashion shop."

"I will have everything made good after we have removed the fittings," Patrick promised.

Jason and Marigold thanked him.

When they had finished viewing and discussing, Patrick asked, "Would you like a drink?"

They asked for spring water.

"My wife is taking me out to dinner," Jason with his arm round Marigold told Patrick.

"Enjoy yourselves, sir and madam."

"I will be in touch. I am very interested," Marigold promised him.

They ate inside the pub this time. The manager remembered them and now Jason and Marigold's friends came regularly. He had prepared them a table overlooking the garden and river. They had a wonderful meal.

Jason encouraged her to tell him about the shop and her plans for it. "We have come a long way from our first time here," he reminisced.

"Yes," she laughed. "If anyone had told me then that I would have eight babies, I perhaps would have run! I wanted a big family, but a big family to me was five."

135

"Have you any regrets, honey?"

"Not for one single moment, my darling husband. Have you?"

"I only regret that I didn't meet you much earlier."

They kissed.

"Come on, sweetheart – time you were in bed!"

"Is that what you were thinking on our first date?" she teased.

"I was, you sexy lady."

Marigold, Philip, Susan, Anna, Maisie and Dianne brought all the children to see 'Mummy's new shop'. Philip took photographs. Customers and staff made a fuss of the children. Marigold and family were so proud of how natural and friendly they were.

Marigold later told Jason, and he said he would have liked to be there.

Patrick told Marigold, "I have heard of a smaller business nearby, and I am going to buy it."

She congratulated him and said she hoped all would be well. She then told him, "Our hairdresser is moving to Turkey to set up a business with her husband. Will you be able to attend to my hair and my family's, Patrick?"

He was delighted. "It will be an honour to help you, Mrs Norton," he said. "Will you prefer me to come to your home?"

"That will be brilliant, Patrick. That is what Gillian did. When will you be able to come?"

"Monday afternoons is usually quiet."

"Right – Monday afternoons it is! Thank you."

Then they all went to buy new shoes for the children. Margaret and Colin chose theirs themselves.

The staff now knew about Marigold buying the shops but they didn't mention it because they felt it was too soon.

Now that Gillian was leaving to set up a business with her husband in Turkey, the staff understood that the family would be supporting the hairdresser near the new shop.

Susan and Anna made sure Marigold had Monday afternoons free. The beautician gave Marigold a body massage with deep conditioning oils and waxed her legs.

Patrick thinned Marigold's hair, but it was still thick and bouncy, as she liked. It gave her a new look. Jason and everyone else were also pleased. The children and Jason also got a new look.

The children loved Patrick – he even trimmed Margaret's doll's hair when she asked him. If Jason was late getting home, Patrick always waited. He went to see the animals with the children and Jenny.

Marigold invited Grace to meet up with her for a coffee.
Grace asked, "Is there anything wrong, darling?"
"No – oh, no, everything is falling into place. I need your advice, please, Grace."

Paul drove Marigold to the coffee house, and he escorted her to the door. She asked him to wait but have a walk if he wished.
Grace was waiting at a table away from the others. They drank their coffee and made small talk.
"You are the first I have asked, Grace: what would your opinion be if I suggest I keep my shop, Yvonne's, and have this solely for teenagers' and children's wear? I have made enquiries and there isn't a shop nearby selling these."
Grace sat back and, beaming, she answered, "If you can manage this, go for it. Your designing these clothes has really taken off. The youngsters and young presenters on the television wear your clothes."
Marigold didn't know that.
Grace went on: "I know because my grandchildren buy your clothes and copy from the television. They are not expensive and they are so comfortable to wear."
Marigold thanked her. "My children are comfortable in the clothes also. They know we don't mind them rolling in mud or whatever, because we tell them the clothes will wash. I am earning a good salary with all my designing plus the wallpapers and curtains. I can afford to keep it."

Walking in the moonlight with Jason, Marigold told him about her idea of keeping her shop for teenagers' and children's fashions.
He said, as always, "You know what you are doing, honey, but will it be too much?"
"Not if I get good staff and a manager. Nearer the time I will put feelers out about staff."
The sale of Miss Grace (the name of Grace's shop) went

through and Marigold kept this shop unchanged. Planning permission was given to put an extension on the back of the hairdresser's. An architect Mr Rudd recommended met with Marigold and her managers.

Marigold had made a list of requirements in advance. The plans were all drawn up and approved, and the workmen got on with the alterations.

Ruth suggested to the local Women's Institute that they invite Maisie to their afternoon meetings. They agreed, and she also went on their short outings with them. Marigold and Jason knew she loved being with them, but they also knew she had been missing her friends and life in Cornwall.

When the newspapers, television and magazines knew that Yvonne's was going to cater for female teenagers and all children, a popular mail-order fashions company asked Marigold to design for them. After carefully considering this and discussing the matter with her managers, she agreed, but she said she could design only children's clothes while she was so busy with other things. They accepted this with grateful thanks.

Christmas was a lovely time at Brierley Manor. Everyone made sure Marigold didn't overtire. Robert couldn't get home this time.

The Gang, Nathan and Peter took the children through the wood and the fields to see the animals.

In the New Year it snowed. Sledges came out for the first time since they had come to Brierley. Snowmen were built with Jason and Marigold's help. Photographs were taken of all these happenings.

Jason rang Maisie two or three times a day when he could whilst at work. He secretly thought he would be very thankful when the babies were born. He was saving leave until after the births. He started planning in his mind for them all to go to Hounscliffe when the babies were about three months old. The last twins had travelled all right, and he knew everyone would help as before. The end of May would be a good time.

He kept these thoughts to himself until he had a chance to discuss it with Marigold.

Michael, the private doctor, and the nurses agreed to come back. They had attended the other births. Brierley Manor was a lovely home to deliver in.

Marigold was getting more tired; the babies were very active, especially when she and Jason had a gentle, short swim. They were obviously going to love water.

Jason put his hand on Marigold's stomach. "Now, you little horrors," he said, "are you going to settle down?" He felt a definite kick! "What have you got in there, honey?"

She laughed. "We'll soon know."

Jason and Marigold didn't use their big bath, but he helped her into their smaller one and washed her hair. Whilst she was soaking he had a quick shower.

When the outside of the new shops had been painted, a special sign was put up. It was a red heart designed by Marigold with the name 'Koki and Tante' in bold lettering. Hanging baskets were put up on either side.

The newspapers, magazines and television all announced the opening with congratulations and pictures. Congratulations, best wishes and gifts poured in from the fashion world, in Britain and abroad.

Jason and everyone else were so proud of Marigold, as always. She had arranged everything while carrying her seventh and eighth children, with calm, dignity and good sense. She wouldn't accept their praises; she couldn't possibly have achieved so much without all of them supporting her.

Chapter 16

In the middle of February she woke up in the night with pains. She didn't disturb Jason at that point, but she lay there praying and thanking God for her coming this far. As the contractions came closer she woke him.

He rang Michael, Maisie and his parents. Maisie informed Mrs Holmes.

The nurses also arrived and they took Marigold into the delivery room. Jason and Maisie stayed with her.

"She is fine," Michael assured them.

Jason was worried but hid it. 'Please, God, let it soon be over for her,' he thought.

God must have answered his prayer, because ten minutes later the first baby was born – a perfect girl. Maisie and Jason silently thanked God. Then, a short while later, the second came out quite quickly!

Jason laughed. "She must be the kicker!"

Again, she was perfect. Thanks to God!

The nurses handed the babies to Marigold, and she cuddled and kissed them, telling them how welcome they were. She handed them to Jason. He kissed her and thanked her. He was crying.

"You are both beautiful," he managed to say. "You are both very welcome."

He gave them to the nurses, who were waiting to clean them up.

Marigold said, "They look like the photographs I have of my mum when she was born."

Jason rang his parents again, then he and Marigold thanked Michael and the nurses.

Michael said, "It has been the highlight of my career, helping to bring your babies into the world. It's a shame these are going to be the last. Next time it might have been quads!"

They all laughed.

"Now, out you go! Your family will be waiting for the good news. I'll call you to come back with the children."

The children were all up and excited. Jason gathered them all in his arms. He was crying.

"I am crying with joy," he told them. "You have two beautiful sisters."

"Where's Mummy?" Roland asked; he started crying.

Malcolm joined in.

"Where's Mummy?" they kept asking. The children then all started crying, "We want to go to Mummy, please."

"We can go up and see her in a few minutes," Jason told them.

Then he, Dianne and Sylvia distracted them. He had a cup of strong coffee. The children had their old toys ready for the babies.

Michael called, "All clear!"

They went up as fast as they could; Jason was carrying Roland and Malcolm.

Marigold was feeding the babies. Jason held all the children to kiss them and their mother. They all stood looking while the babies suckled hungrily and made noises.

Marigold laughed. "That's not very ladylike," she said.

They suckled until the breasts were empty. Jason was taking photographs; he sent them to his parents, who promised to come with Anna and Trevor before the men went to work.

Jason rang and told his PA that he would now be taking his leave. His colleagues had been expecting this call, and they and Jason had prepared for it.

Marigold showed the children the babies. They gave them the toys.

Marigold thanked them. "They can't talk yet," she said.

Jason then said, "Mummy has to rest now. Come on, little horrors – let's go and get some breakfast. Your sisters have had theirs."

They just stood. They didn't want to leave.

Jason, looking at Marigold, then told them, "You can have the day off school; I will play with you and take you to see the animals. We can come back when Mummy has had a sleep."

They were excited about that, and they went down with Jason. Dianne was waiting for them.

Jason said, "I have suggested they don't go to school today. I hope you don't mind."

"No, sir, they would never settle with the excitement."

"I'll just go and freshen up," he said. "Then we'll have breakfast. I have promised I will take them to see the animals. I will spend time with them today."

"Thank you, sir. I will ask if I may help Mrs Norton."

Maisie then came to help Dianne.

When they went outside there was a crowd at the gates. Jason and the children went down to see them. Ned and Ruth were there with other people from the village. They all congratulated him and Mrs Norton on the birth of their twin daughters and said they hoped they were all well.

"Yes, thank you," Jason replied.

He passed his mobile round, showing pictures of the babies. Everyone was very pleased all was well.

Jason thanked them for their concern and good wishes. "The other children are having a day's holiday," he said. He thanked them again and said, "Bye for now."

He and the children ran off until they came to a grassy slope, out of sight of the gate. The children started rolling down and Jason joined them. They landed in a heap at the bottom, laughing,

"Again, Daddy, again!"

He obliged five times more, then told them, "Come on – the animals will be waiting to hear about your sisters."

Jason went to see Marigold whilst the children were washed and changed; he got a parcel out of the cupboard. Marigold had bought a present for each of the children from the babies, as she had done before. They were on their own; the nurses were in the bathroom.

Jason kissed her and said, "Good, brave girl, my precious girl, I adore you more and more."

He gave her a jeweller's box. Inside were the most beautiful necklace and earrings, decorated with small stones in all the colours of the rainbow interspersed with small diamonds. The sunshine caught the diamonds. Marigold was speechless with wonder.

"I designed these specially for you, honey."

She cuddled and kissed him. "They are magnificent! Thank you, darling husband. But I haven't bought you anything."

"Well now, the best present you will give me will be in a few weeks' time."

They laughed with joy.

"Most certainly! You have my promise."

"Yes, honey, but you know what we discussed: I am having the snip, and that is final. If you get broody again, go and talk to the animals!"

She laughed. "I think we will be busy enough with eight children."

They thanked God for the safe delivery and their eight beautiful children.

The babies woke and the nurses came in with them.

"May I?" Jason asked.

They nodded.

He picked them up and cuddled and kissed them.

"You are very welcome, little daughters," he said. "Your mummy, brothers and sister and I love you both very much."

They started yelling! He gave them to Marigold. They were craving for her breasts; she began feeding them.

"May the children come for five minutes, please?" Jason asked the nurses.

"Certainly they may, sir."

He fetched them. He and Marigold gave them their presents from the babies. They loved the presents and thanked the babies.

Jason said, "Their names are Yvonne and Juliet."

They all said, "Thank you, Yvonne and Juliet."

Jason said, "Come on – the babies are having their lunch. Let's go and have ours."

"Yes," they all shouted.

Yvonne and Juliet's eyes followed their voices.

"See you later, honey. Have a good rest."

"I will. Bye. See you later, children."

"Bye, Mummy, Yvonne and Juliet."

Jason sent a photograph of the twins with a message to his colleagues in the office, his gang, Robert and then Nathan and Peter.

Ned met up with his pals and told them about the new twins being girls. He did on this occasion buy them a pint each!

Whilst the children had a rest, Jason went back up to Marigold and the babies.

"Look in my wardrobe, darling," Marigold told him.

Hung there was his missing old jacket plus a new, black, soft leather one. He gasped and put it on. It fitted perfectly across his broad shoulders. He held his old jacket up.

Marigold laughed. "Yes, darling, I borrowed it. We took it to pieces to copy. We won't need to do this again; we now have your pattern!"

He tenderly held her in his arms. She knew he was overwhelmed by her thoughtfulness.

"You are – you are the most, honey! Thank you very much. I love it."

She teased: "For your birthday would you like a dark green?"

"I would, please."

He then left Marigold to sleep and took the children swimming in the shallow end of the pool.

Jason loved and was proud of his new leather jacket. He took great pleasure in telling his colleagues and gang how Marigold and her staff had taken his old jacket to pieces to make this."

They all said, "Wow! She obviously loves you very much."

The private maternity nurse arrived to take over. Michael came in the late afternoon to make sure everything was all right. Jason walked him to the car.

"Your wife has done marvellously once more," he said. "She still has a very healthy womb, but perhaps she will need a bit more rest this time. No running off to the shops until next week at least!" he joked. "You are a lucky devil, Jason." They were friends.

"I am, Michael, and I thank God."

Michael laughed. "I never thought I would hear you say that, Jason."

"Well, there we are. Now, Michael, as you know, we discussed me having the snip – will you please arrange it?"

"Now, don't be hasty," he teased. "Just think – next time it may be quads!"

They laughed and shook hands.

"I wouldn't be surprised," was Jason's parting shot.

Jason took the children up for the last time that day. They had a lovely time. The children had drawn pictures of the babies, and Marigold kept them with her.

"Now, darlings, Mummy has to rest again."

Colin asked, "Did Yvonne and Juliet come out of your tummy?"

"Yes, they did, like you all did."

"Like the animals?"

"Yes, well done! That is correct, Colin."

They all started chattering about the animals. Jason took them downstairs, and later he and Maisie helped Jenny bath them and put them to bed.

Jason went for a stroll with Maisie before dinner. They discussed the birth, the children and the babies.

Smiling at him, Maisie asked, "I hope this is the last time. I don't think I can stand any more."

"You will not have to, Maisie; I'm having the snip before Marigold changes her mind and gets broody again."

"You are terrible, Jason. Fancy telling a spinster something like that!" she teased. She thought the world of him and admired him greatly.

Jason then said, "I haven't discussed it with Marigold yet, but I have been planning in my mind when, we could go back to Hounscliffe. Malcolm and Roland were only three months old when we travelled. The end of May should be a good time. What do you think, Maisie?"

"I think that sounds good. You have the furniture set up. Supplying Yvonne and Juliet's needs will not be a problem. 'Koki and Tante' should be running smoothly with the managers."

Philip, Susan, Anna and Trevor had been with Marigold. They came down and Jason ran up and had a quality time with her before dinner. He went back up afterwards. Brenda was in the nursery with the children.

"Would you like me to stay with you? I could sleep in the daybed, honey; I could carry you to the bathroom?"

"Thank you, darling, but Maisie will stay with me and Brenda is next door, so you go and get a good night's sleep. You didn't get much last night. I have to walk a little, you remember."

"Yes, I do – but ring me if you need me, sweetheart."

"I always need you, Jason."

"Thank you. I always need you too. I'll go and let you sleep also. See you in the morning, honey. You look beautiful."

She could see he was reluctant to leave, but, out of respect for Maisie and Brenda, he went. When he had gone she lay thinking about him and what he had done over the day: how he had been with her at the births, as he had with all the other babies; and how he had taken the children to play rolling down the slope. She nearly laughed out loud when she thought how this gorgeous, charismatic Queen's Counsel, because the children wanted him to, had told the animals about the baby sisters. She lay there tingling all over with sheer love and gratitude, for him, her beloved husband and the father of her children. She prayed for each one of them, including the last two, who waved their arms about. 'They must have been doing that in my womb – all that activity,' she thought. Marigold laughed to herself again. 'They have probably inherited French genes!'

Next day the children went to school and nursery.

Miss Gladwin told Margaret and Colin's class that they had two new sisters. "They have brought photographs for us to see," she said.

Colin piped up: "They came out of Mummy's tummy just like animals do!"

There were only a few in the private class, including GP Mary's two children.

"Yes, that's correct, Colin. Perhaps you would all like to draw your favourite animals." This distracted them from what Colin had revealed.

She discussed this with her colleagues at lunchtime: "We need to look at this carefully; even though they are only six years old, they are intelligent and sensible enough to be told about nature and birth."

146

When Jason brought Margaret and Colin back for the afternoon, Mrs Mason, the headmistress, told him what Colin had said.

He listened very intelligently and agreed. "It's easy for Colin as he sees the animals almost daily. Do the other children get the opportunity?"

"I doubt it," Mrs Mason replied.

"Right, when you have their parents' permission, what about bringing them to see the animals whilst I am on holiday for a few days?"

"That is a very excellent idea, Mr Norton. Please leave it with me."

The school secretary wrote a note which was duplicated and handed to each pupil to take home:

> Dear Parent,
> We have been invited by Mr Norton to go to Brierley Manor to see their animals. If you approve, I will then discuss with the children how animals and babies are born.
> Do you approve or otherwise. Please reply as soon as possible.
> We could go whilst Mr Norton is at home for a few days with Mrs Norton, who has recently given birth to twin daughters.

All the parents approved and welcomed this; it was a wonderful way to introduce the children to the facts about birth in a most sensitive, intelligent way.

The children told their parents and nannies that Colin had said his sisters came out of his mother's tummy.

"Yes, they did; that's how you were born. You are going to see Colin's animals with Miss Gladwin and Mr Norton on Friday. You will need to take your wellingtons. It may be muddy."

They all sent a card (apart from Mary, who took their card and presents personally), congratulating Marigold on the safe delivery of her daughters; and they thanked her and Mr Norton for allowing their children to come to see the animals and to begin to learn about birth. They all said the same thing: 'The only problem is that now we are expected to keep animals and produce twins!'

Jason said to Marigold, "Good old Colin, eh?"

They laughed.

"I would like to have seen Miss Gladwin's face when Colin said what he did."

"Yes, I would too," laughed Marigold.

The villagers knew that Mr and Mrs Norton were not snobs. Although Marigold and Jason sent their children to a private school and nursery, they played with village children in the park, and they had frequently been brought down to the village ever since they were babies.

Jason and Paul fetched Miss Gladwin and the class for the Friday morning visit to Brierley Manor.

All Colin and Margaret's friends loved the animals – even the pigs that smelt slightly! They wanted to collect the chickens' eggs, but they were too late.

Jason promised, "Another time – either early morning or teatime."

As they went round, Miss Gladwin explained to the children how the animals were born. Jason was very impressed.

They went back to Brierley Manor, where Mrs Holmes and Maisie had drinks and home-made biscuits ready for them. When they had had this break, Brenda and Jason carried the baby twins down in their carrycots, and Miss Gladwin explained that they had come out of Colin and Margaret's mother's tummy.

The children all understood.

Jason and Paul took them back to school and waited for Margaret and Colin. The school and the parents were very thankful for this sensitive teaching. In the lunch hour, Miss Gladwin told her colleagues about the visit. She said that it had been a 100% success, and she hoped Mr and Mrs Norton would continue these visits. They were all certain they would. They then went into a discussion about how gorgeous Mr Norton was.

Jason and Marigold again received letters from all the parents thanking them for the visit and the opportunity to see the babies.

After experiencing the kindness of the community, who had gathered at the gates waiting for news of the twins' birth, Jason suggested to Marigold, "We should invite the village to a party."

"A garden party – it will be summer."

"Yes. Our lawn will be ruined, but it can soon be regrown."

"Do you think we will seem to be patronising them?" Marigold asked.

"I hadn't thought of that. I wouldn't think so. Shall I ask Ned?"

"Good idea! Ned will tell us the truth."

Ned and Ruth asked around: "Would the village like to attend a garden party at Brierley Manor? What about a Saturday afternoon in early July?"

They were all certain that they would. Ned's pub pals asked if there would be a beer tent.

Ned promised there would be.

"I would like all of us to go to Hounscliffe at the end of May for two weeks, if you agree, honey. Will that be too soon for you? The shop will be up and running by then. We went when Malcolm and Roland were three months old, and we haven't as much to organise this time. We were still getting set up then. There will be extras for Yvonne and Juliet, naturally."

"Of course, darling. Does the family know?"

"I put feelers out, but we are waiting for your approval, of course, honey."

"Yes, it will be lovely, darling Jason."

"The garden party could be in early July, so we can go back to Hounscliffe in early August if you want."

"That sounds wonderful to me, darling. I will support you in every way I can – you know that."

"I do, honey sweetheart."

"We will be able to book the caterers and hire portable loos. Do you think we ought to order a large marquee in case it's raining?"

"That's a brilliant idea, honey. We'll check the long-range forecast first."

"I suppose they will expect alcohol."

"We need to ask Ned about that as well!" Marigold laughed. "Do you think we ought to make him our general manager?"

"Well, with his pension we wouldn't have to pay him much."

They laughed.

Marigold said, "Come here, you." She held him close. "I don't want our time together to go too fast, but I will be very glad when the twins are six weeks old."

"Whatever do you mean?" he teased her.

They both laughed.

"It's now time for me to feed the babies."

They were lying contentedly in their cot. Jason carefully lifted one, then the other, and passed them to their mother. They were eager to drink her milk. He stood gazing at the three of them.

Marigold began to design a dress to match the rainbow colours of her necklace and earrings. She created a colour for the material to highlight these colours then interspersed small flowers in the colours of the rainbow. When it was made up it was absolutely marvellous. The designers wanted to copy it, but Marigold didn't allow them just yet. It was very special to her. They understood when they knew about the jewellery Jason had designed for her.

The producer of the television chat show on which Marigold had last appeared asked her to give him an interview about the new shop. Jason encouraged her to agree, and the crew and presenter came to Brierley Manor as Marigold was still breastfeeding Yvonne and Juliet.

They recorded in the morning when the light was good, but they set their own lights up too.

The programme opened with photographs of Marigold with Philip, Susan and Anna looking at the shop after coming out, and Marigold viewing with Jason and then going into the pub to buy her husband dinner. She then answered questions.

"Yes, Grace gave me the opportunity of buying her shop as she was retiring."

Marigold talked briefly. "My managers and I had been discussing the possibility of moving into larger premises as the business, Yvonne's, had grown so much. We discovered there was an opportunity of buying larger premises at the side of Miss Grace. This is a real blessing for us. We are able to spread out and display our fashions in the larger windows."

"Is it true that the shop is in Mayfair?"

"Yes, Miss Grace will remain as a textiles and haberdashery store, which will be very useful for us. It also sells gentlemen's and ladies' ready-made wear. We will be able to alter these clothes if they don't fit. I have kept the same staff; Mrs Preston is the new manager. This is a great help to me."

"Is it true that you made all the arrangements and negotiated the deal when you were in the last stage of a pregnancy which resulted in your fourth set of twins?" he asked.

Marigold's face lit up. "Yes, I did, but with my husband and everyone else's support and help I bought it and named it in honour of my mother, Koki, and my aunt, Yvonne." She started crying and apologised. "Hormones!" she exclaimed.

They all laughed.

"Bereavement never leaves you, does it?" he sensitively asked.

She shook her head.

He asked her more questions and she answered in her beautiful clear voice. She made them laugh.

"Is it true that your paternal and maternal grandparents and your parents left you financially secure?"

"Yes. I am very grateful for that, and that is why I have always sought good advice and take care not to squander. Also, because of their love and caring, making sure I had money, I worked extra hard at school and university."

"They would be very proud of you now."

"Thank you. I hope so."

"You call the new shop Koki and Tante."

"Yes, and I pray I will make a success of it. I am very grateful to my managers, including Mrs Preston, and all my staff. They are trustworthy and faithful. It is not just a means of earning money to us, but we are proud that we are serving people and bringing trade into this country."

"Will you have an October show, Mrs Norton?"

"Yes, we are looking forward to this."

"Is it now time for you to feed your babies?"

Marigold blushed and laughed. "It looks like it."

The camera showed Brenda with both babies in her arms – they were yelling!

A lady brought Marigold the most beautiful bouquet of flowers; she thanked her and the crew. Then the presenter gave her a small box. The camera zoomed up close. It was a small gold brooch with 'Koki and Tante' embossed on it.

She was crying again. She looked up and tried to thank them. They all clapped her.

The camera went back to the babies, who were still yelling.

Marigold stood up.

Marigold had a notice put in the newspapers and magazines and on the television, announcing that Yvonne's would be closed until mid-July. For the time being the business would be transferred to Koki and Tante in Mayfair. When the shop reopened, selling children's and female teenagers' fashions, it would be renamed '0–19'.

Staff and a manager will be needed. Apply with health, school and police reports, also qualifications and samples of work and designs.

All the family went to Hounscliffe at the end of May. The travel arrangements were as previously. Maisie travelled with them.

Marigold and Jason had asked her once more to live with them, but she wanted to go back to her friends and life near Polzeath. They respected her for that. She promised to come up for Christmas if they were not coming to Hounscliffe.

Marigold told her they would definitely be spending Christmas at Brierley, but they would come to Polzeath for part of the long summer break. Ned would care for the animals as before. Also, the family would often come for weekends and holidays.

They had serious discussions about the garden party. Thankfully, the outdoor pool had been fenced off so that nobody could fall in, but there were many other matters to consider: Did beer taste all right in polystyrene cups? Did they want a Punch and Judy show? Should dogs be invited? Did they want a brass band?

Jason suggested they ask the schoolteachers' opinions.

Ned was asked about the beer, and he said, "We could try it in polystyrene cups; then we will know."

Marigold asked, "Why not enquire if there is someone who organises garden parties?"

They all seized on that. It would take the strain and stress off them, particularly as they were extra busy just now. Also they resolved to keep a record of all aspects of the organisation, as that might prove to be a great help in the planning of future events.

Trevor looked on the Internet and came up with three names of professional events organisers. They interviewed the three and chose the man who lived the nearest.

They settled on the first Saturday in July from 2 p.m. to 4 p.m., before 0–19 opened and before their holiday in Cornwall. The schoolteachers, Jason and Marigold's new friends, Nathan and Peter, Robert if he could make it, the Gang and the WI all promised to help the family. Ned, of course, was the overseer. His pub pals offered to be in charge of the beer tent, and this was gladly accepted with Ned's approval. The Gang agreed to organise rolling down the slope. Someone was needed to keep their eyes open so that the village children didn't let the animals out, and Jason naughtily suggested the headmistress, Mrs Mason!

Chapter 17

The owner of the mail-order company asked Marigold if her children would model clothes in the new book.

She thanked him, and said, "No. With me designing, this would be inappropriate. But if my husband agrees, you could advertise, 'As worn by Mrs Norton's children'.

He was pleased with that.

Jason agreed. "I see no harm in that, as you have designed the clothes."

Marigold drew comic designs based on their own animals for the children's materials to be made up for the shop. Colin also drew his ideas of rabbits and other animals from his imagination. These were not copied in any way from books. Marigold was thrilled. She, naturally, didn't put any pressure on him, but she was proud of him and told him so. She told all the children how proud she was of them.

When Marigold returned from Hounscliffe her PA had been swamped with requests for a job. There were four male applicants who were finishing college at the end of June. They had passed all their exams in design, art (including graphic art), cutting-out, machining, and machine knitting. When they came for their interviews, they brought their college and school reports as well as police and health checks. These were all excellent. They were clean, hardworking and trustworthy. The college mentioned in Frank's report that he had potential managerial skills, which should be encouraged.

"This is unusual," Marigold remarked, "young men doing this work."

Jason pointed out, "Honey, it is only like men being ladies' hairdressers, designers or PAs."

"Yes, of course. You are right, darling."

Marigold and her managers shortlisted and interviewed the four young men first. They were very impressed with their appearance and manner. Marigold discerned that Frank had the qualifications and charm to be the manager. He also was talented at arranging displays. Marigold studied their abstract designs; she recognised their talent and quality.

She had a discussion with Pauline and Helen whilst the men were shown over the shop. (They were very interested in everything.) They came back and they all had a coffee.

Marigold told them, "I thank you for applying; we are very impressed with you and your skills. May I now speak with Neil, Anthony and Michael?"

Pauline, Helen and Frank left the room, and she offered the three men jobs in 0–19. She suggested a salary to begin with; they were very pleased.

"Now may I have a word with Frank?"

Frank came back in, looking a little anxious.

"Sit down, Frank." She smiled at him. I have employed your three friends, Frank, and now I offer you the position of manager of 0–19. All your skills will be used. These will help me very much.

He thanked her for this opportunity and promised, "I will not let you down, Mrs Norton."

She suggested his starting salary. "Is this satisfactory, Frank?"

"Thank you very much, Mrs Norton."

"Will you please ask your friends to come back in?"

They all came back, smiling and looking pleased. They realised that working for Marigold and her businesses would be a wonderful opportunity.

"I have offered Frank the manager's job," she said.

They clapped.

Marigold laughed. "Frank will also be in charge of all the displays, particularly the windows. His other skills will also be used. The shop will open the third week in July. After a three-month trial, if satisfactory (which I am positive you all will be), I will review your salaries. 0–19 will be closed all day Monday and Wednesday afternoons."

They thanked her.

"Have you time now to choose your sewing and knitting machines and everything else you will need on the Internet?"

"Yes please, Mrs Norton. We would like to have the same models as we used in college. They incorporate the latest technology."

"Order the latest-design suitable computers for your work."

Marigold rang her PA, Lindsey; she had warned her that she might ask her to help the new designers to order equipment.

"Would you like a drink?" she asked them.

"Yes please, Mrs Norton."

Val organised this for the computer room.

"We will attend evening classes beginning in September to gain more expertise, Mrs Norton," Frank told her.

"Good."

"When the machines and everything are set up I would like you to begin making clothes for us to have ready for the opening. I have some designs and materials ready."

"We will be able to do that, Mrs Norton," Frank said. "Now we have passed our exams we can leave college at any time."

"Is this satisfactory for you?"

They all nodded.

She shook hands with them. "What had you planned to do now?"

"We're going to have a game of squash, Mrs Norton. If we hadn't got the job, we could work our frustrations out on the court."

She laughed. She liked these young men.

"We're meeting friends this evening for a pint," Neil said.

She laughed again. "Now you have jobs, you will be expected to pay."

"Oh, we hadn't thought about that," said Anthony with a laugh.

"This is a brilliant start to our careers," Frank said.

They all agreed.

Maisie and Julia had brought the babies for their feed, and Marigold retired to her private office.

The next day Marigold and the managers interviewed their shortlist of three girls. They were all bright, enthusiastic and had good school reports. They had excellent health and no police records. She asked Heather to wait outside. Val was waiting, she offered her a coffee or non-alcoholic drink.

Vivien and Kathy had worked as sales assistants in a clothes department store for two years, they both had a satisfactory report from that store. They told Marigold they and the store knew that 0–19 would be a greater challenge and opportunity for them. Marigold offered them the jobs; they accepted with joy.

"Please ask Heather to come in."

Heather came in and was invited to sit down. Marigold, Pauline and Helen smiled at her.

"Heather, I have studied your abilities, and now we have larger premises I am offering you a position in this shop, designing and making casual and formal clothes for nineteen- to twenty-five-year-old ladies. Please think about this, Heather, and then contact me."

"I don't need to think about this, Mrs Norton. I would love to do this work. I will be using all my training skills and I love fashion."

"We will advertise this new beginning. I would also like to enter outfits in our October show. Would you like machines like those you have used at the college?"

"Yes please, Mrs Norton."

"Right, also choose the latest-design computer to help you."

Marigold told Lindsey about Heather's needs.

"You mentioned that you were continuing your studies at college in September. In view of your working here full-time, I would like you to attend a one-month five-day-week course at Westfield. It's a private college. I will pay. You have a unique gift for designing and it will be to my benefit as well as yours to set this up. Just now they have two vacancies. Are you happy with this, Heather?"

"I feel very honoured, Mrs Norton."

"Right, I will set it up for you to begin next Monday. You will receive your wages plus travel expenses. I'm going to ask Anthony to attend with you. I am not showing favouritism. Each one of you has a special gift and I would like to nurture it. I must feed my babies now, Heather."

"Thank you very much for this opportunity, Mrs Norton. I won't let you down."

"I am positive you will not, Heather."

They shook hands.

Marigold told her, "My PA will contact you about coming to see me on Friday morning to finalise arrangements for Westfield and draw your contract up."

When Marigold had fed the babies she texted Frank, telling him what Heather would be doing – including her going to Westfield for a one-month course beginning the following Monday. "I would like Anthony, if he is willing, to attend with her," she said. "He will be paid his wages, and I will pay his fees and travel expenses."

Frank was delighted. He knew Anthony had a special talent for designing.

Marigold then asked Frank if he and Anthony could make an appointment with her PA for Friday morning to finalise this matter and draw Anthony's contract up. "Also, Frank, as you will be working full-time, instead of you, Neil and Michael going to college in the evenings, what about you all going on Mondays whilst the shop is closed? I will pay your wages for the day as well as the fees."

"Thank you, Mrs Norton. This will be brilliant. A full day is better than just an evening."

"I will set this up," she promised. "I have a bright Saturday girl for you, Frank. See if she shapes up."

Frank thanked her again for everything she had done for him, and on behalf of his friends.

Paul was waiting to take her, Maisie and Julia home.

After lunch Marigold went to rest. She was tired but pleased with the outcome of these interviews. She decided to spend the following day at home. Before she went to sleep she again wondered how on earth she could manage without her faithful staff. She knew she couldn't. They all enjoyed their jobs, but she decided to give all of them a bonus.

Nelson was getting old now, and he hadn't the strength to go for long runs. He was content with short walks and slept the rest of the time. Jason was very tender with him, making sure he had the nourishment he needed, and giving him food he could manage to eat; he knew he was nearing the end. He nursed him on his knee, thanking him for all the pleasure he had given them and for being a good friend.

When Nelson died peacefully, Jason and Marigold cried. Marigold told the children, and she couldn't stop crying again.

She explained, "Nelson hasn't been able to walk far lately and has wanted to sleep. Now he is asleep for ever."

Colin – bless him! – asked, "Will I go to sleep for ever?"

"Yes," Marigold told him, "we all will when we are very old and tired, like Nelson was." She cried again. The children gathered round and cuddled her. She told them, "Daddy is very sad. We must think of doing something very lovely for him. What do you suggest?" They stood looking at her and thinking.

"Shall we roll down the slope?" David asked.

"Yes, yes! Please, Mummy, roll down the slope!" they all shouted.

"All right, we will ask Daddy if he wants to."

"He will! He will!" they shouted again.

Yvonne and Juliet woke.

"Will you draw a picture of Nelson for Daddy?"

"Yes, we will."

They fetched their books and crayons.

Jason managed to get home a little earlier. After greeting Marigold, Yvonne and Juliet, he ran upstairs to the children, who showed him their drawings of Nelson.

He started crying. They all cuddled him.

Colin said, "Don't cry, Daddy. Nelson is only asleep."

Jason realised that Marigold had explained to them. His heart warmed. "Yes, he is. That's correct."

He helped Brenda and Marigold prepare them for bed, and he read each one of them a story. When they were asleep he and Marigold went down.

"Thank you for explaining to the children about Nelson dying, honey. It's part of their education and life – birth and death! Now we have to think about where we will bury him. Shall we involve the children?"

"I think so, darling, to complete their understanding. Otherwise they might expect him to wake up and be here again. Shall we bury him in the flower garden and plant a rose bush?" Marigold asked.

"Good idea, honey! We will be able to visit his grave and keep him alive in our memories."

Marigold promised to buy a rose bush next day.

Later, when they were soaking in the bath, Marigold told him, "We were trying to think of something to cheer you up, and we all thought we could all have a roll down the slope?"

Jason smiled. "We'll arrange that, but in the meantime I am thinking of you and me in a different *roll*."

Marigold laughed. "You are cheeky!"

Next morning, Jason told the children about the idea of Nelson being buried in the garden and about planting a rose bush called Nelson on the top.

Margaret said, "We can visit him, Daddy."

"Yes, we can, darling. Now, what's this about all of us having a roll down our slope?" he said, looking at Marigold with the special look he had for her.

She blushed.

Their friend James, the vet, took Nelson until Saturday morning.

Jason was in the final stage of preparing a court case for Monday, so he stayed late on Friday (as he often did when this was OK) to make sure Saturday morning was clear.

All the family came up – except Robert, who couldn't make it. Ned joined them. John the gardener had dug a hole; Jason gently lowered Nelson in.

The children put their drawings in and said, "Bye, Nelson. Thank you."

Marigold moved them away whilst Jason and John filled the hole and planted the rose bush. They all stood for a few minutes then went down to the slope.

They all took it in turns to roll down – even Ned. They took photographs for their family album. Ned didn't tell his pub pals about this! He would never have heard the end of it.

Jason rang James to thank him for helping them with Nelson. James told them he had heard that a litter of Labradors was expected at a nearby kennels. The owner was a reputable pedigree breeder who had the welfare of the dogs at heart. Labradors are gentle dogs and they are patient with children.

"How many are there in the litter?" Jason asked.

"At least seven – do you want them all?"

"Mrs Holmes and the other staff would leave if we had all these! What about a couple of dogs? Could they be house-trained before they come here?"

"This can be arranged."

Mrs Holmes gave her approval. "You shouldn't ask me, sir. We are so happy being here that we will help all of you with anything."

"Thank you, Mrs Holmes. We know and appreciate that, but two will be enough for now. The vet did say there might be seven."

"Good gracious!" she laughed.

"I would have liked to join in a roll," James told Jason.

"Right, what about a Saturday afternoon soon?"

"Will Rita be able to come?"

"Yes please."

Rita, James's wife, was a vet and partner in his business.

"We'll see if Bill and Mary and their children are able to come at the same time. Who said life in the country was dull?"

James laughed. "It was before you lot came!"

Jason asked Michael, their doctor, and he promised to come if he possibly could.

All those invited agreed to meet on Saturday afternoon at 2.30 for the rolling down the slope and then afternoon tea.

On the Monday morning Colin and Margaret stood at the front with Miss Gladwin as she told the class their dog, Nelson, had died.

Colin said, "He fell asleep; when we are very old we will all fall asleep."

Miss Gladwin hastily broke in: "Yes, children, when we are very old, we die."

She asked Colin and Margaret to sit down, and then she

161

encouraged the other children to tell if any of their animals had died. They responded with tales of goldfish, cats, mice and hamsters. They were going on to talk about grandparents and other relations so she had to call a halt, but she was very relieved this had passed without any of them being upset.

Colin put his hand up.

She thought, 'What is coming next?'

"Yes, Colin?"

"Miss, after we buried Nelson in our garden, Daddy and John planted a rose bush on the top."

"We called this rose bush Nelson," Margaret said.

"That's lovely, Colin and Margaret. When we come to our art time, would you all like to draw a picture of your favourite animal or a rose?"

Colin then said, "Miss, after we planted the rose, we all rolled down our slope – Granddad and Grandmamma and everybody, but not Mummy because she feeds our new sisters."

Miss Gladwin thought she had better quickly move on!

During lunch she shared all this with her colleagues.

"Isn't it wonderful that they are learning about birth and death so naturally?" Mrs Mason, the headmistress, said. "Whatever shall we do when Colin and Margaret go to their next school?"

Miss Gladwin reminded them, "There are six more of them to come."

They laughed.

"They will keep us on our toes," Mrs Mason said.

They all agreed.

Someone then said that if she were married to Mr Norton she wouldn't mind having so many children. "Do you think they will have more?" she asked. "They haven't been a problem to Mrs Norton – carrying them and delivering."

They went quiet at that.

Miss Gladwin told them, "Margaret said her father was crying when Nelson died, so her mother suggested that to cheer him up they would all roll down their slope. Imagine a famous brilliant barrister crying over his dog dying! He will make a wonderful compassionate judge, won't he?"

They again all agreed.

Mrs Mason wrote a letter to Jason and Marigold:

We were so sorry to hear that Nelson has died. We are grateful to Colin and Margaret for sharing this with us. Miss Gladwin is very thankful also that Colin and Margaret encouraged her class to talk about dying in a natural, non-frightening way. They have recently learned about birth and now they have discussed death.

We all hope you are feeling better now, Mr Norton, after the rolls down your slope.

Marigold and Jason also received sympathy cards from the parents of other children in the class.

They enjoyed their usual Saturday-morning family walk through the wood, though Nathan, Peter and Robert couldn't make it this weekend, unfortunately. Jason wheeled the twins in their pram. Margaret wheeled her doll's pram. Then they had their usual good Saturday lunch.

After lunch, before the friends came for the rolling down the slope, Jason had a quiet word with Marigold. "Will you arrange for Dad, Trev and Anna to help bathe the children? I need to have a private word with Mum."

"Of course, darling. Is there anything wrong?"

"There is something."

"Leave bath time with me, Jason."

"Thank you for that, honey."

Trevor joined in the rolling, but Philip, Susan and Anna volunteered to take photographs for the family album! Marigold was resting after feeding the babies.

Marigold, Yvonne and Juliet joined them for afternoon tea. They sat outside at the tables under the shade. Members of the Women's Institute helped Mrs Holmes and Martin to prepare and serve this. They were glad of the wages, which they put towards taking senior citizens on coach trips.

Everyone enjoyed themselves immensely. Jason invited them to come again to see the gardens and animals. They all welcomed this invitation.

Chapter 18

Jason asked his mother to have a stroll with him; they walked arm in arm.

"Now, Mum, there is something bothering you. I am not a trained barrister for nothing."

"We have been going to tell you and Marigold. Lynden is now much too big for us. Also, with Dad retiring, shortly we will not have his salary. We are financially secure with Trevor always looking after us, and Dad will get a good pension, but living where we are is pricey." She started crying.

They sat down on a bench.

"There is no problem. You know Marigold and I would love you to live with us – not to be made use of, but to have you near. You would have your own rooms of course."

"Darling Jason, it isn't that. Thank you, but we want to be on our own. We are still young. We will be selling Lynden and buying a smaller home.

It will be large enough for Nathan and Peter to come to; Robert, as you know, is getting married. But Dad and I are worried about what you might think about our selling the home you were brought up in. We will be depriving the children from coming and playing in the wood."

"They have this wood, Mum. Bricks and stones are not important as such; it is human relationships that matter. You and Dad will be more comfortable in somewhere smaller. Lynden is very big. The vital thing is for you and Dad to be happy where you live. Dad has worked hard all his life. He has always been on call unless he was away on holiday. Are you sure that is all that's bothering you? Are you or Dad not well?"

"We are both well, darling. We go for regular check-ups. Dad's blood pressure is sometimes high, but now he is winding down that problem should be solved. We did wonder if you and Marigold would like to move there."

"I can speak for us both when I say, no, Mum, we love it here. We are all settled. It is further away for us to get to work, but that is no problem. Thank you for asking, darling."

"Well, that's settled then. We will ask Matthew to help us find something smaller and more suitable. Then we will put Lynden up for sale. All kinds of doubts have been going through our minds. It is a good job we have Trevor! He soon puts us right."

They laughed.

"Promise me you will not worry about anything, but look forward to your new beginning whilst you are still young enough to enjoy life to the full."

"We will, darling. However, we may not have room for the horses."

"Right, that needs some thought; they could come here of course. Let me talk with Marigold about this, Mum."

"We had better go and help with the children."

"Sit here another ten minutes, or do you prefer to walk?"

"No, I am fine here, Jason, thank you."

"Please don't spoil Dad and Trevor's fun with the children; they grow up so quickly. Look at your sons, Mum! Where would you like to live, Mum?"

"If at all possible, near to a golf club," she answered promptly.

He laughed. "Ask a stupid question! Do you mind if I start putting feelers out? Look how I got to know about Brierley. I am positive you will hear of a home that meets all your requirements, Mum. There is no rush, is there?"

"Now we have decided to move, we want to get things settled, darling."

"I understand that," he said. "Come on, then, Mum – if you are ready, let's go and rescue Dad and Trev."

"All right, darling. You are a good son. I should have known nothing would escape you. I am so sorry we hurt you and Marigold."

He put his finger on her lips and shook his head. "Why don't the four of you go to Amelia and Geoffrey's for a little holiday?"

"We would love to when we have our new home organised. We keep in constant touch with them, as does Marigold. They love receiving pictures of the children. We often laugh about when you and Marigold went to view Brierley; none of us expected eight children! They are so beautiful."

He laughed. "I think Marigold would like to have a hundred!" She agreed.

They walked back arm in arm.

"I feel more positive now, Jason."

"Look, Mum – Marigold and I are here for you. Whenever you want to talk to us in private you only have to say."

Malcolm and Roland were fast asleep. The family were reading to the other children. Marigold was sat in an armchair contentedly cuddling Juliet and Yvonne. Jason had a word with his father and Trevor, and they arranged to meet for lunch when possible once a week in London.

When they went downstairs Jason fetched two bottles of his very best red wine and they shared with Marigold about selling Lynden.

She told them, "If during the changeover you want to stay here, you will be most welcome."

They thanked her.

Whilst Marigold was feeding Yvonne and Juliet, Jason told her, "Mum and Dad will be getting rid of the horses, honey."

She looked at him. "What are you thinking, darling – bringing them all here or just your horse?"

"Nero is getting old now. I had such good times with him; I don't like to think he will be unhappy."

"No, have him brought here. Shall we buy Willow and Kizzy (they are in foal) and Brandy for you to ride? There is room in the fields, and we have the stables. We will also be thinking about ponies for the children, won't we?"

"Yes, honey."

Melvin was a brilliant horseman. He was in his early fifties and he had had a good job. His wife had left him ten years previously, and, with the stress of his job on top of this, he had had a nervous breakdown and suffered 'nerves'. Melvin was an educated, decent man, and he loved horses. He had been a showjumper when younger. He liked to keep himself to himself now.

Philip had heard about him at the golf club, and, knowing he wanted an outdoor job with not much responsibility, he had offered him the job of caring for his stables. He lived in a large caravan on the estate. He had begun to write a detective story, and he had had a book of poems published.

He asked Sir Philip, "Will Mr Norton need me to continue caring for the horses?"

Jason and Marigold discussed this, then Jason had a word with Ned.

"I can't see any problem, sir. You have known him for a few years."

Marigold told Jason, "Let's take this opportunity. You will have peace knowing he is caring for your Nero."

"Yes, I will be happy with that, darling."

So it was arranged for Nero, Willow, Kizzy and Brandy to come to Brierley Manor. Jason and Marigold bought them from Susan and Philip. They wanted to give them, but Jason said, "That wouldn't be fair on my brothers."

Melvin had his caravan moved to the top of the fields, away from the pigs! He quickly made friends with Ned. Although he had previously been a loner, he now had a cooked breakfast and lunch every day with Ned and Ruth. He wrote his story in the afternoons.

Ned told Marigold, "Horse manure will be marvellous for your roses, Mrs Norton."

Marigold laughed.

When Jason and Marigold were soaking in their bath, Jason said, "I never realised, until Mum asked me if you and I wanted to buy and live in Lynden, how isolated it is – set apart. I wasn't aware of that when I was growing up in it. I suppose I was too busy being educated. Perhaps I never would have realised if my eyes hadn't opened to what we have here: a beautiful home, the woods, the fields, and, more importantly, we are surrounded by a wonderful community. We belong to them." He went quiet. They were both deep in thought. "And now Mum, Dad, Anna and Trev are part of it with us."

"Yes, sweetheart. I understand exactly what you are saying. We are not isolated. We are so busy that we probably wouldn't realise it if we were, but we are in the heart of the village here and I love the surrounding area."

They went quiet again.

"I am learning so much through other people, honey. Textbooks and book-learning are vital, but it is learning about emotions and what makes people tick that is vital. I have increased my understanding of life through the people here, and this is helping me in my work."

"Yes, I do fully understand, Jason. You will make a wonderful, compassionate judge."

Not for the first time he asked her, "Where would I be without you, honey? Come on – let's get out. The water is going cold."

"Any excuse!" she teased him.

The Gang were preparing to marry their police officers. Marigold took great delight in designing their dresses as well as Margaret's. (She was a bridesmaid for Sandra, who was marrying Daniel, the police inspector; the boys were pageboys.) Marigold also designed the boys' suits. The whole family was so proud of the children and how they behaved so responsibly. Sandra's family's children were in their teens.

Before Kathleen agreed to marry Robert, she told him, "I love you very much, but I don't want children."

His heart sank, but he continued to listen.

"I love your brother's children – they are brilliant – but I have just been promoted. Until I met you I was set on being a career woman."

He knew she loved him. He offered to leave the army because he was away from home so much.

She asked, "Do you really in your heart want to?"

"No, but I will if that is what you want."

"No, darling, it isn't. I am so proud of you."

Robert was naturally disappointed not to have children, but he hid his feelings. He had Jason and Marigold's children to visit, and no doubt the Gang would have children, and so might Nathan and Peter when they married. He also realised that it wasn't always easy for children whose father was away from home for long periods. So he settled his mind: at least he would have Kathleen to come home to. Apart from loving each other, they were the very best of friends. She had taken his loneliness away.

They slept together. She didn't want a white wedding, but not because she wasn't a virgin; she just wasn't a white-wedding person.

Marigold designed her a beautiful tailored two-piece with a pillbox hat and a small veil. A small spray of flowers decorated her handbag. She looked radiant and beautiful. Robert was very proud of her.

Whilst Jason and Marigold were having a stroll on their own, he said, "Honey, we are so lucky our children so far are healthy and obviously intelligent! Lots of children are in need. I am dealing with a case in which the parents have a little girl who was run over through no fault of her own. She now needs specialist education to stretch her brain. They have not had much luck."

"We could ask Ned in confidence if there are any needy children in this area."

"Yes please, honey. I would like to try to help them in a non-patronising way."

"You are a good man." Once more she told him, "You will make a brilliant judge." She kissed him very lovingly.

Thankfully the garden-party Saturday was sunny. The organisation had been hectic, but everyone communicated and the groups of helpers knew exactly what was expected of them. Six portable toilets were erected. Hundreds of chairs and plenty of small tables had been borrowed from the village hall. Members of the St John Ambulance came in case any first aid was needed. A local policeman joined in the fun.

Clarissa, Linda and their husbands came with the children. They all enjoyed themselves. The local vicar and his wife also came. He asked Jason if his children would like to attend Junior Church. Jason promised they would when they were a little older. He told him his friends came on Sunday mornings.

To that the vicar responded by saying they would all be welcome.

169

The events organiser was excellent. He brought in a children's entertainer but no Punch and Judy. They had a bouncy castle, and they had difficulties keeping the adults off it.

The local ice-cream van came. Trevor asked Jason, "Should we ask for commission?"

Jason laughed. "I doubt it."

A brass band played. Some chairs were put in front, and others were spread around in circles. The catering company provided lovely refreshments. The beer tent was popular – especially with Ned's pub pals and the landlord. Celebrities and film stars who were Marigold's customers came and signed autographs. Patrick and his wife also came.

Ned and his pals had one roll down the slope. That was enough for them! The Gang and a couple of police officers oversaw this rolling. It was the most popular event of the afternoon.

All the helpers gathered at the gates to say goodbye. Everyone said it had been a marvellous afternoon. They didn't want to leave, but they knew there was going to be a repeat next year. The Women's Institute and teachers handed out a balloon and apple to every child.

Roland was asleep in Jason's arms. All the children were tired, as were the adults!

Jason and Marigold thanked the events organiser and booked him again for the next year. They thanked the helpers. They all said it had been a lovely time and they would feel flat now it was over.

Jason told them, "There is next year!"

Philip, Jason and Trevor had formed a good relationship with Clarissa's husband, Roger, and her father, Matthew. Jason invited them all to join in their Saturday or Sunday morning walks. They accepted this with gratitude. Matthew and Philip arranged a game of golf together.

Everyone left but Philip, Susan, Anna and Trevor, who had offered to help Brenda bathe the children whilst Jason stayed with Marigold feeding the babies.

When Jason told Marigold about inviting Roger and his family, he apologised: "Sorry, darling, I should have asked you first."

"Certainly not, dearest! This is your home. I do hope they come."
She then hesitantly asked, "Did you have a fling with Clarissa?
Jason, please tell me the truth."

"The absolute truth from my heart, honey, is that thankfully I
did not. She asked me, but that's as far as it went. That is why
when she met you she was so jealous and bitchy."

"I can't really blame her, darling; you are so dishy. I would
have been the same if you had rebuffed me."

"But you never asked me, honey, before we were married."
He laughed. "You've asked plenty of times since, and I don't
remember ever turning you down!"

"You are the limit, Jason Norton!"

He pulled her on to his knee and asked, "When are the family
going home?"

0–19 was off to a successful start. Frank was a brilliant manager.
He had the idea of asking the teens and children what styles
they would like to wear. Marigold gave him permission to 'go
for it'.

Frank put a big cardboard box just inside the shop for
suggestions. They were overwhelmed with requests for more fun
logos, especially on the tee shirts. They also received some very
good ideas, which helped them.

Marigold, after getting Frank's permission, teamed Anthony with
Heather at Koki and Tante. She employed one of Frank's friends,
who was talented at producing logos and fun embroidery. It was a
very popular, busy shop.

Susan and Philip were told of a suitable home. Lynden was sold
for an outstanding price. They gave each of their four sons a lump
sum.

Jason bought an eight-seater BMW X5 to take Marigold and
the children for a run on Sunday afternoons; it was also used for
going to Hounscliffe. He bought Marigold a six-seater Mercedes.
He had specially adapted seats installed for taking the children to
nursery and school, or going to Marigold's shops. He used
Marigold's BMW for work. The remainder of the money they

invested with Trevor after giving a donation to the charities they regularly supported.

They all went to Cornwall and went to see Mrs Haslam and pick up Betty, of course. She had knitted a present for each of the children.

At the café, the waitress laughed again. "Eight now!"

It was a fantastic three weeks. It rained some days, but that didn't stop their enjoyment at all.

Matthew and Linda made enquiries about buying a holiday home near Hounscliffe for the next year. Clarissa told Roger, "We had better get on making a brother or sister for Sonia."

When she told her parents about this, Matthew looked at Linda, who said, "Thank you, darling, but I am happy with Philip, and my grandchild and future ones."